Praise for About a Rogue

D1554454

Praise for A Scot to the Heart

Also by Caroline Linden

What a Gentleman Wants

What a Rogue Desires

A Rake's Guide to Seduction

Other Novels

What a Woman Needs

Novellas and Collections

When I Met My Duchess in At the Duke's Wedding

Map of a Lady's Heart in At the Christmas Wedding

A Fashionable Affair in Dressed to Kiss

Will You Be My Wi-Fi? in At the Billionaire's Wedding

Short Stories

A Kiss for Christmas

Like None Other

Written in My Heart

HOW THE SCOT WAS WON

Desperately Seeking Duke

CAROLINE LINDEN

Caroline Linden

Copyright © 2021 P.F. Belsley

Cover © 2021 Erin Dameron-Hill/EDHGraphics

Image: Illustrated Romance

Editor: Eve Silver/Edits by Eve

ISBN: 978-0-99714949-4

For Rebecca

Acknowledgments

Many thanks to Catherine Stein and Dabney Grinnan, as well as several of my Facebook readers, for helping with the Latin. Any mistakes are entirely mine.

Prologue

Agnes St. James was her father's favorite child.

Some of her earliest memories were of bouncing along atop his shoulders as he did errands around Edinburgh. Her mother protested, but George St. James just laughed and took Agnes to the Exchange, to his banker, to visit merchants. He taught her to ride their pony astride, without her mother's knowledge. He taught her to swim in the firth, this time with her mother's approval. He took her on long walks in the nearby countryside, and even taught her to play golf and cricket with her older brother Andrew and his friends.

But her favorite place to go with Papa was the family's silk shop. He had bought it when she was a small child. By then Drew was in school and her mother was home with her two little sisters, Winifred and Isabella, so Agnes got Papa all to herself at the shop. He would sit her on the counter and let her touch the shining bolts while he told her where the silk came from and how it was made.

Agnes loved the shop. She loved running her fingers over the beautiful, delicate silks, imagining them made into lovely gowns and frock coats. She couldn't wait to stand behind the counter and unfurl a roll of silk before someone's rapturous gaze, the way Papa did.

Papa was delighted by her interest. "That's my clever girl," he would exclaim as she figured yardages and costs on her slate for him. By the time she was ten, Agnes had come to think of the shop as her future, and she spent hours daydreaming of how she would arrange the window displays and the salon, when it was hers.

A month after she turned twelve, Papa developed a cough. Mama begged him to stay in bed, but he insisted he needed to work. Agnes, by then allowed to come to the shop every afternoon, listened as his cough grew harsh and hacking.

The doctor came, but no tonic or poultice helped. In a matter of weeks, her hearty, active father sickened and wasted away until he simply didn't wake up one morning.

Agnes was devastated. Mama wept until she fainted. Bella, almost eight, started sucking her thumb again, and Winnie wouldn't come out of her room. Heartbroken, they buried him in the neat churchyard of St. Mary's, only to discover that it was just the beginning of their nightmare.

Papa had not been good with money. In fact, he'd been quite bad with it, and now they had none—less than none, as there was a mortgage against the shop. Drew returned from the lawyer's, white-faced and solemn, and told Mama they were actually rather poor.

Agnes grew up five years in one day when Mama, pale and quiet, put on her second-best dress—now dyed black—and went to take over the shop, leaving Agnes in charge of the house and her sisters with only the help of Annag, their sole remaining servant. She spilled soup on the floor, her sisters had a screaming fight that brought the neighbor to inquire what was wrong, and when Mama finally came home Agnes fled to her bed in tears.

The lowest moment, though, was the day Agnes arrived

home and found Winnie eavesdropping at the parlor door, her ear pressed to the wood. "There's someone here to see Drew," she mouthed to Agnes, who scurried over to join her. The voices were coming closer to the door, and the two girls ran up the stairs to avoid being caught.

The door opened. Out came a man about Papa's age, then a younger man. That was Felix Duncan, Drew's friend, who played cricket and golf with them. Drew followed, his head bowed. The man paused, speaking to Drew in a low voice.

Felix glanced up the stairs and saw them. Winnie gasped and fled. Agnes stayed where she was, her heart racing.

She knew Felix. He was the sort of boy who never backed down from an argument, who played hard until the last batsman was called out, who regularly was scolded for his smart mouth. Papa liked him immensely; "a good lad," he'd said, even when Felix and Drew got into trouble together.

Today Felix gave her a long look, then a quick nod, as if to say, *don't worry, all will be well.*

When the visitors had gone, she crept down the stairs. "What did they want, Drew?"

Her brother looked far older than eighteen. "Mr. Duncan offered to help with Papa's affairs, and then he offered a loan."

"How much?" she whispered. That must have been what Felix's nod meant, what a good friend indeed he was—

He sighed. "I can't take it."

"Why not?"

"What we need is money," Drew said bleakly. "We already have enough debt."

Three days later Drew accepted a lieutenancy in an army regiment being formed. A fortnight after that he was gone, leaving them with his first month's pay and a promise to send more when he could. Mama told them they must bravely wave good-bye to him and not cry, but Agnes spied the tears on her mother's cheeks as her brother disappeared up the street.

Agnes and her sisters began going with Mama to the shop, sweeping the floors and tidying the workroom. There were no more hikes on Arthur's Seat, no more cricket. No one else came to call. They moved house twice to smaller and cheaper lodgings. Her brother was gone, her mother worried nonstop, and if not for the kind but anonymous neighbor who left a ham or joint of meat on their step every month, they would have gone hungry at times.

But they still had the shop. It was the only thing that carried her onward. It was her link to Papa, her hope for the future, and Agnes vowed she would make it the best in all Edinburgh.

FELIX DUNCAN WAS his father's pride and joy.

There were five other names in the family Bible, three before his and two after. Only one of those sons had lived longer than a year, and Felix didn't remembered any of them. Felix was all his father had left.

At times it was wonderful. He never had to work for his father's attention; every day at breakfast and dinner he had it. No matter how petty or small his complaint or victory, his father listened. If a tutor made Latin or mathematics confusing or dull, Lachlan Duncan would explain it patiently until Felix understood.

The Duncan men went into law. They all had for four generations, with the exception of one cousin who inexplicably became a merchant captain. Felix always knew he would be an attorney, from the time he had to stand on his father's law books to see over the desk and watch Lachlan write a brief.

He always told Felix what he was writing. "Mr. MacDonald was arrested for murdering a man behind a tavern," he would explain, "but he has been falsely accused."

"How do you know?" It was his father's favorite query to him, and Felix loved to turn it around on him.

Lachlan was pleased when he did. "Firstly, because he swore an oath that he did not. Secondly, because his wife and his landlord saw him at his home on the night his friend was murdered. And thirdly, because the poor soul who was killed was seen gambling that night with another man, and had accused him of cheating for all to hear." Lachlan tapped his nose. "That casts serious doubt on the charge that Mr. MacDonald would hurt a man known to be his friend."

"And that other man killed him?"

Lachlan would raise a finger. "I don't have to answer that, son. I only have to show that Mr. MacDonald did *not*."

But at times, it was not wonderful to be the pride and joy. Sometimes it was a millstone around his neck. When he grew bored under a strict tutor's hand and ran away into the alleys and closes of Edinburgh, or was caught sneaking the brandy, there was no one else to absorb his father's temper.

Once he complained to his friend about it. "Damned unfair of my brothers, to leave me to carry on the Duncan honor myself," he grumbled.

"Aye," agreed Andrew St. James. "The redheaded runt of the litter. Your poor da." Which started a wrestling match that Felix won only by dint of refusing—ever—to cry pax.

St. James never disappointed his father, Felix was sure. Drew was the image of *his* father: tall and athletic, good-humored and amiable. Unlike Lachlan Duncan, who was often in court or the Advocate's Library at Parliament Square, George St. James had time to umpire cricket matches and hike the nearby hills. If Felix didn't quite want to *be* a St. James, he wouldn't have minded if his father were more like Drew's.

Until Mr. St. James died suddenly.

That was terrible. Felix only dimly remembered when his

own mother died, when he was five. But Felix didn't realize how terrible it was until Drew said he could not go to university that fall after all.

They had expected and planned to go together. It was unthinkable that Drew wouldn't; he was a lord's grandson, and belonged at university. Something had to be done.

His father was surprised by his request. "Help the St. Jameses?"

He nodded. "Mr. St. James died last month. They're in a bad way."

"Ah," murmured Lachlan. "What do you propose?"

Felix opened his mouth, then hesitated. "There must be something we can do…"

His father waited.

"There are three little girls, see," he explained. "And the widow. Drew doesn't see how they can survive if he goes to university."

His father's eyes narrowed, but he nodded. "Very well."

It didn't go as planned. Drew flushed when Lachlan offered funds, and failing that, legal advice. "Thank you, sir, but I think I've got it."

Felix's father didn't let go easily. He quizzed Drew for half an hour, before sitting back with a nod. "If ever you need it, my offer remains."

"Thank you, Mr. Duncan." Drew jumped up to show them out.

Felix was deeply frustrated. In the corridor he caught sight of two of the little girls spying on them; one ran but the other stayed, her wide blue eyes anxious.

That was Agnes, the tenacious one who used to come along to the cricket pitch. Her father always let her play. She was too small to bat, but she was fast in the field. And she never ever gave up trying, which Felix admired.

He couldn't disappoint her. Felix gave her a confident nod.

"What else can we do?" he demanded outside.

His father's stride didn't break. "Nothing."

"What? Why?"

Lachlan looked sharply at his indignant outburst. "He's got pride. He won't accept help."

"Yes, but... What will he *do*?"

His father stopped. "He's your friend, aye?" On guard for a trap, Felix nodded slowly. "Then do him the courtesy of trusting him. He's a grown man—too young to support a family, but it's his decision to make. I can't tell him what to do." He gave Felix a speaking look. "He's not *my* son, is he?"

No. Drew was not. But Felix was, and so Felix watched helplessly as his friend joined the army and left Edinburgh. That fall he went to university and studied law, as planned. He kept an ear out for the St. James family, but their shop remained open, and the girls looked healthy the few times he spied them. Drew must have figured everything out, as Lachlan had predicted.

But he never forgot the little girl with the big blue eyes.

Chapter One

❦

Twelve years later

Mr. Agnew's coffeehouse near the Exchange was a favorite of the legal set, being near the Justiciary Courts and the Advocates Library. Felix Duncan spent nearly every morning there in search of breakfast, frequently returning in the afternoons for business, and sundry other times when he had nothing better to do. Agnew brewed the best coffee in Edinburgh, and his wife Martha was a divine cook.

On this fine spring day, he sat with William Hunter, with whom he shared a law office, ostensibly to discuss a brief regarding a client's case, but in reality to pass the time with plenty of hot coffee and cakes before being called to present the case. Under normal circumstances he would have been relaxed and unhurried; the case was well in hand, and he expected to win his client's argument. There was also a lively discussion going on about the rash of robberies that had afflicted the town of late, as attorneys made a parlor game of guessing the defense one might make.

Today, Felix wasn't aware of any of it.

He had been earlier, but then he'd turned around upon Hunter's arrival and spotted *her*. Ever since, his eyes had wandered back toward her repeatedly, until even Hunter noticed.

"You're staring." Hunter folded back a corner of the brief and made a mark. "Again. I'll begin a tally."

"If you would finish that brief, we could leave," he retorted, though he was in no hurry to go. The woman across the public room was lovely. He'd never seen her here before, and he would have noticed. She sat in a ray of sunlight that had forced its way into the coffeehouse solely to illuminate her, making her dark curls shine and her pink jacket look like a freshly picked rose. She picked up her teacup and sipped, glancing his way in the process. For a moment their gazes connected.

Felix grinned involuntarily. Her eyes widened uncertainly. He dipped his head in silent greeting. She turned back to her companion.

"I'll finish the brief later," said Hunter, watching over the rims of his spectacles. "Don't let me keep you from more pressing matters."

"No, no, read it now," he said. Helen, the girl who served the pastries, stopped by the table, *her* table, and the ladies spoke to her.

"You're in a sad state." Hunter was openly mocking him. "I'll send the Buchanan brief over tomorrow, aye? When your mind is available to concentrate on it?"

"Right," he murmured, still mesmerized.

"And I'll charge my next tavern round to your account."

"Aye." The lady in pink gave Helen a beaming smile, and his breath caught. By the saints, she was a beauty.

"Might have my horse reshod and send you the bill for that, too," went on Hunter.

"Mmm-hmm," he said absently. Helen was nodding, and

now headed toward the kitchen, which lay directly behind his table.

Felix put up a hand as she approached. "Good morn, Helen."

"And to you, Mr. Duncan." She grinned. She knew him well, as he practically lived here. "More coffee already?"

"Did those ladies happen to order some of Martha's currant buns?"

She looked puzzled. "Aye."

He gave her his most engaging smile. "Would you deliver them to my table instead, so I might deliver them to theirs?" Helen frowned in suspicion. "I'm acquainted with the lady by the window," he added hastily.

"Then why don't you go say a word to her without needing a plate of buns to smooth your way?"

Hunter snorted with laughter.

Felix held up a shilling and tried to look angelic. "Have pity on a fellow, Helen…"

"He needs help," put in Hunter. "Too timid to speak to a woman without an excuse."

Felix made a rude gesture at his associate. Helen rolled her eyes but took the coin and departed for the kitchen.

His partner was watching with raised brows and a fiendish grin. "Are you really acquainted with her?"

Felix resolutely refused to turn around again, unlike Hunter, who was all but staring at the women now. "I am. Well, in a manner of speaking. I know her brother."

Hunter's brows shot up. "Mrs. Ramsay's got a brother? No, she doesn't."

"Not Mrs. Ramsay, idiot," said Felix under his breath. Hunter was speaking far too loudly. "Her companion."

Ilsa Ramsay was the daughter of a prominent tradesman. Her wealthy husband had died a year ago in a duel made all the more infamous by the lurid trial that followed it, but instead of retiring in privacy, she had burst out of mourning, months early, like a butterfly from a chrysalis. Edinburgh was both scandalized and intrigued. Today she wore a gown of vivid yellow and a warm, friendly smile that caused more than one man in the coffeehouse to pause and watch her.

But not Felix.

"What?" His friend's face went blank with surprise, and he craned his neck for another look. "Not Mrs. Ramsay? Oh... Now I see."

Anyone with eyes could see. The other lady was quieter and more simply dressed, but just as striking. Felix fought off the urge to look her way again. "She used to come along to the cricket pitch when we were lads. Her brother was a crack batsman, and her father would umpire the matches. She was only a child the last time I recall meeting her, but now she's..."

"Certainly not a child," finished Hunter when he fell silent. "Aye, she's very handsome."

Felix fervently agreed. "Are they looking this way?"

Hunter snorted with laughter. "Nay, lad, they've no idea you're alive."

Cautiously he peeked over his shoulder. The ladies had their heads together over a magazine on the table. As he watched, the lady in pink picked up her teacup, the steam visible in the sunlight. She pursed her lips and blew on it before taking a sip, and Felix's stomach tightened. By God, what a lovely mouth she had.

Helen reappeared and set down a tray holding a plate of warm currant buns and a crock of butter. "Go on with you," she told him. "Make haste."

Felix grinned and leapt to his feet. "Merci, Helen. Hunter, wish me luck."

His partner leaned back in his chair and folded his arms. "You'll need it! I've never seen such a hopeless case."

He ran one hand down his front, smoothing his waistcoat,

and picked up the tray. "I appreciate your confidence." And he headed toward the table by the window.

"WE ARE BEING SPIED UPON," murmured Ilsa Ramsay.

"Hmm?" Agnes St. James didn't look up from the magazine, busy reading the description of a magnificent gown worn by a countess to an opera in London recently. It would make a splendid window display in the silk shop, if she could recreate it.

"Over there," Ilsa whispered with a slight nod. "Tall, ginger hair, commendable shoulders. He is staring."

Oh. Agnes smiled briefly. Another man struck by Ilsa. She'd been friends with Ilsa for four months, and this happened regularly. "Be kind to him," she whispered back.

Ilsa looked hurt. "Am I unkind?"

Agnes grinned at her. "You determinedly turn away every man who tries to flirt with you."

Her friend made a face. She had only been widowed a year ago and had often declared she didn't want another husband. That didn't stop men from pursuing her, obviously. "Only the ones I know. They are suspect."

Agnes turned the page. The countess's hat was described as well, to her delight. "Do you know this one?"

Ilsa tilted her head, making no effort to hide her observation. "No," she said thoughtfully. "But he is very handsome."

Agnes shook her head, smiling ruefully, and reached for her tea. Oh, to be a single lady in possession of both beauty and a large fortune, able to entrance men from across a room.

"Oh my. He is coming this way."

"That didn't take long," Agnes murmured.

Ilsa rolled her eyes before assuming a bright smile as a man stopped beside their table. His kilt swung as he made a sweeping bow.

"I beg your pardon, mesdames, but have you ordered some fresh currant buns?"

His voice was lovely. Agnes glanced up at him through her eyelashes. As Ilsa had said, he was tall and handsome. Decidedly so. And vaguely familiar. A frown touched her brow. She was sure she knew who he was...

Ilsa regarded him impishly. "We did! But has something ill befallen Helen? Has Mr. Agnew pressed you into his employ?"

He laughed. "Not at all! Poor Helen is frantic, nearly run off her feet, and I hastened to offer my services in her moment of distress."

As one, Agnes and Ilsa looked past him to see Helen watching, hands on her hips and a smirk on her face, clearly not frantic at all. "How very considerate of you to leap to her aid," said Ilsa drolly. "If we were acquainted, I would thank you by name, sir."

He laughed again as he set down their plate of buns and butter. "It would be my pleasure to tell you. Felix Duncan, at your service, madam."

Agnes's eyes widened in surprised recognition. *Oh.* Involuntarily she looked up.

His eyes were fixed on her. His smile grew wider as their gazes met. "Forgive me—Miss St. James, is it not?"

The breath caught in her throat. Ilsa turned on her, eyebrows arched. "Yes."

"Why, what brilliant luck," he said in delight. "You surely don't remember me, but I attended Mr. Cruickshank's school with your brother Andrew."

"Oh..." She couldn't seem to say anything else. She did remember him, and not for attending Mr. Cruickshank's.

"Did you really?" Ilsa exclaimed. Agnes could tell she was enjoying this turn of affairs. "How fortuitous! Did you not say your brother is returning to town soon, Agnes?"

Mr. Duncan's face brightened. "Is he? That is excellent news."

"It is," said Ilsa warmly, even though she had shown no interest in Drew's visit before. "Would you care to join us, Mr. Duncan? To renew your acquaintance with Miss St. James?"

Agnes glanced at her in astonishment—and dismay.

Mr. Duncan seemed to see it. He smiled ruefully. "Thank you, madam, but I wouldn't want to intrude. Indeed, I've surely disturbed you enough already."

"Not at all," protested Ilsa. "We are ever eager to hear new conversation and gossip."

He hesitated, and Ilsa kicked Agnes under the table.

Reluctantly she raised her eyes again. Mercy, he was tall—much taller than the gangly boy she remembered. He'd grown up very well, nicely filled out with magnificently broad shoulders. His hair was less violently ginger now, more of a rich copper, curling in a neat queue. Square jaw, narrow nose, generous mouth.

Like all her brother's friends, Mr. Duncan was a good six or seven years older than she. He and Drew had got into a great deal of trouble together, for which Mama mostly blamed Felix Duncan. He'd been fearless and boisterous, with a sharp wit and a quick tongue. Papa had been fond of him, though. If asked, Agnes would have sworn up and down that he wouldn't remember her.

Remarkably, it appeared he did.

"Please, sir," she said, to avoid another kick from Ilsa.

Instantly he pulled out the chair beside her and sat down. "How is your brother? I've not seen him in years. Is he still in the army?"

"Yes." Agnes still wasn't certain what was happening. "We expect him for a visit within the month."

He grinned. The tiny lines crinkling around his blue eyes hinted that he smiled a lot. "I shall hope to encounter him."

"I don't know how long he plans to be in town," she said quickly. "It's rare he has leave from his regiment."

She didn't add that none of her family knew *why* Drew was coming to town. He'd written to them several weeks ago saying that he'd been urgently summoned to England by their distant cousin, the Duke of Carlyle. Mama hoped it meant a legacy; she'd begun to despair of the smokey chimney and the loose windows in their sitting room. Agnes has seen her reading listings for the fine new houses being built in the New Town, sighing over the cost.

Her brother's next letter only made Mama's hopes soar. He wrote that he had news and was coming to Edinburgh, which was far out of his way back to Fort George. "It must be *very* happy news," Mama had said joyously.

Mr. Duncan sobered at her words. "I wouldn't want to keep him from his family. Would you convey to him my cordial regards?"

Ilsa gave her a sly look. "Perhaps you will invite Mr. Duncan to tea, Agnes, so two old friends can meet again."

Agnes was so surprised she laughed. "*Drew* wouldn't come to tea! He'd slip away to the links at the first rattle of teaspoons."

"Clever man!" Ilsa had just learned golf and was always ready to play. "Perhaps we could form a group."

"The last time we played golf you brought Robert, and he ate Bella's ball," Agnes pointed out. Her youngest sister had been angry at first—no doubt thanks to the peals of laughter from Agnes and Winnie—but gave it up when Robert approached, head hanging, to nibble at her elbow. Bella loved animals.

Ilsa smiled at this reminder of her pet's misdeed. "He did indeed," she said fondly. "I shall leave him at home when we play with the captain, Mr. Duncan."

Mr. Duncan's warm regard hadn't wavered from Agnes.

"It would raise the stakes considerably if there were a chance of someone eating a ball."

Ilsa laughed. "Indeed! Robert is a pony. There is always a chance of him eating something."

"I see." Mr. Duncan grinned. "But here—I have kept you from Martha's excellent currant buns." He rose from the chair. "It was a delight to make your acquaintance, Mrs. Ramsay. Miss St. James..." He turned toward her, his smile warming and his voice dropping a register. "It was a great pleasure to see you again." With another elegant bow, he turned and walked back to the table he'd come from, where another man sat watching as if they were acting a scene upon the stage.

Agnes reached for a currant bun, her heart unaccountably racing. She applied herself to buttering the bread, hoping Ilsa would go back to the magazine still open between them.

"Are all your brother's friends so handsome and charming?" Ilsa was watching Mr. Duncan with unabashed interest.

Agnes snorted. "No! At least, I expect not. Drew's not here enough for me to know who his friends are these days, let alone judge their charm or appeal."

"Pity." Ilsa nibbled her currant bun. "He's still watching you."

Agnes flushed. "Is he?" She took a quick bite of her bun, sighing with pleasure at the taste of the tender bread, still warm from the oven.

"Like an owl, very still and unblinking with his head turned all the way around, no doubt thinking he's invisible."

She choked on the bread. "Don't be ridiculous!"

"No? Look for yourself."

Licking butter off her lower lip, Agnes stole a glance his way.

He was watching, just as Ilsa had said. And when he caught her peeking at him, he grinned and tipped his head.

She jerked back around, her heart skipping.

Ilsa was gloating. "It was unclear whom he wished to flirt

with when he first approached, but now there is no doubt at all."

Agnes took another bite to keep from answering. That seemed implausible. In the four months that she and Ilsa had been friends, no one had ever chosen to flirt with her instead of with Ilsa. And it made complete sense: Ilsa was beautiful, rich, and widowed, while Agnes was...not.

"He said it was a delight to meet me, but it was a *great* pleasure to see you." Ilsa leaned forward, her eyes dancing. "The man is smitten!"

Agnes took a sip of tea. "Nonsense. He knows my brother..."

Ilsa scoffed. "A pretext! How eagerly he leapt at the suggestion of a golf outing."

Agnes smiled in relief. "Golf! That's not flirting. An afternoon shouting at each other over the wind, stomping through the marsh in search of wayward balls, arguing over a drop."

"But he might stand very close to be heard over the wind. He might offer to carry your club. He might ask you to choose his ball."

"Pssh." Agnes's face was burning. "If he needs my help there, he's no one I wish to golf with."

Ilsa looked disappointed. "He most certainly wishes to golf with you."

"I will only go if you bring Robert." Agnes dabbed the butter from her mouth. "I would very much enjoy watching Robert bedevil my brother and his friends—who were, in all my memories, incorrigible rascals."

"Perhaps they still are." Ilsa wiped away her sly smile at Agnes's aggrieved look. "I am only teasing, of course. If you don't like him, I shall never mention him again."

Agnes refused to answer. She turned back to the magazine. "Oh look, there is a new poem."

Ilsa gave in, and they spoke no more of Mr. Duncan.

· · ·

BUT THE NEXT time they went to Agnew's, he brought their buns again, along with choice gossip. There had been another robbery: the thieves had stolen a large load of tea from a grocer the previous night. They spent an hour coming up with increasingly humorous ideas to catch the thieves, and never even opened the magazine.

The third time, Agnes found herself hoping to see him. She scanned the room as they entered, but he was not there. Disconcerted, disappointed, she followed Ilsa to a table. But then the door opened and he burst in, out of breath, searching the room just as she had done. When their gazes met, his face lit up, and an unexpected tide of delight filled her.

"Were you running, Mr. Duncan?" Ilsa asked as he approached.

"A very brisk walk." He gave Agnes a wink. "In case they should run short of currant buns."

She smiled back at him. "We must order extra today."

"The way to my heart," he declared with a laugh, which sparked a giddy feeling inside her that lasted the whole day.

By the fourth time, Agnes knew he would be there. Now she and Ilsa always went to Agnew's, abandoning all the other coffeehouses and tearooms. Mr. Duncan was waiting. No sooner did they sit down than Helen set the tray in front of him, and he brought it to their table.

"Mr. Agnew *should* hire you," said Ilsa in admiration. "What service!"

He laughed. "I'm only a lawyer, madam, not qualified to supplant Helen."

"Oh yes, your father was a lawyer," said Agnes without thinking.

He looked at her with such delight, she blushed. "You remember," he said softly.

"Yes."

They might have gazed at each other forever if Ilsa hadn't cleared her throat.

He started. "Excellent. Erm… What is your opinion of the new Assembly Rooms?"

Agnes bit her lip. The Assembly Rooms, recently opened in the New Town, were the talk of Edinburgh. But they were also expensive, and the St. Jameses could not afford the subscriptions.

Ilsa hesitated. "They are glorious."

Mr. Duncan was watching her. "Have you been, Miss St. James?"

She smiled wistfully. "I hope to see them someday. Will you describe them?"

And he did, patiently answering her every question.

When they left, Ilsa linked her arm through Agnes's. "The truth," she demanded. "Is he not charming?"

Agnes smiled. "He is."

"Handsome?"

"Indisputably."

"And?" her friend coaxed.

Agnes blushed. "It's only flirting."

"Very persistent flirting."

But nothing more. Mr. Duncan had never said a word about calling on her, nor asked to walk her home. Agnes had begun to wish he would. "It's nothing but a lark."

Ilsa only smiled. "We shall see."

Chapter Two

As it happened, Agnes got to see the Assembly Rooms much sooner than expected. They returned home one day to find a packet containing four tickets for the ball the next evening.

"Who sent them?" Bella cried as Winnie clapped her hands in joy.

Each ticket had to be endorsed by the holder to be transferred, but the signatures were illegible. Mama shook her head. "There's no message. Oh, if only we knew whom to thank…"

Agnes suspected. Ilsa knew how much she and her sisters longed to go, especially after the conversation with Mr. Duncan.

The next day was a storm of preparation, sponging gowns and mending hems and fighting for the mirror. Winnie took so long with the curling tongs that Bella threatened to cut off Winnie's strawberry blond locks in retaliation, and Mama threatened to put the tickets in the fire.

Agnes was every bit as excited as her sisters. She wore her best dress, a pale blue chemise à la reine with a gauzy white ruffle at the neckline, and touched a drop of scent on her throat. Perhaps Mr. Duncan would be there—a thought that made her smile at her reflection, and then run down the stairs when her mother called that the carriage had arrived.

Though new, the building exterior was unimpressive, and the interior still smelled faintly of sawdust and paint. Winnie and Bella expressed their disappointment as they climbed the stairs. At the top, Agnes turned and whispered, "Behave! Mama won't let us come again if you're rude."

Winnie rolled her eyes. "Thank you, Agnes, for telling us what we already know."

"Have some faith," added Bella with an impish smile.

Agnes gave her a stern look. "Prove me right to do so."

Winnie made a face. "I intend to have a splendid time, Agnes. I hope you can unbend enough to do the same."

"Don't worry about me!" She laughed. "I know how to enjoy myself and not get into trouble."

They had reached the main ballroom, and here all argument ceased. Even devoid of decoration, the room was splendid: high-ceilinged, twice as long as it was wide, illuminated by dozens of candles, and filled with elegantly dressed people. There was an alcove above for the musicians. Mama gave them permission to go and headed toward a clutch of respectable matrons.

Within minutes Winnie and Bella had found friends. Agnes looked for Ilsa, and then Mr. Duncan, but saw neither. Finally she spied Sorcha White by the far fireplace, surrounded by gentlemen. Sorcha was Ilsa's friend, but Agnes had met her several times.

"Agnes!" cried Sorcha as she drew Agnes to her side. "You must all meet Miss St. James," she told the gentlemen around her. "Someone fetch her some wine."

Almost instantly someone presented her with a glass, making Sorcha laugh in approval. Agnes sipped, feeling bold and daring.

"Is Ilsa here?" Agnes wanted to thank her for the tickets.

"I'm sure." Sorcha gave a coy glance at the nearest man—an officer, from his coat. "There will be dancing, and *everyone* adores a country dance, don't they, Captain?"

"They do, Miss White." Openly admiring, the officer seized Sorcha's hand. "I shall adore it even more if you stand up with me for the first set."

Sorcha agreed, which spurred another gentleman to beg the second dance. Forgotten, Agnes scanned the room. With a start, she saw her sisters holding no fewer than four gentlemen enthralled. Winnie was three years younger than Agnes at twenty-one, and Bella had just turned nineteen. Perturbed, she finished her wine.

"Captain Aytoun!" Sorcha plucked Agnes's glass from her hand and held it up with hers. "We are out of wine!"

Grinning, the officer stopped a passing waiter and handed full glasses to Agnes and Sorcha. Agnes hesitated, then accepted it as Sorcha raised her own glass in salute.

Ilsa arrived, which increased the merriment of the group considerably. When the musicians took their places and the first dance was called, Ilsa and Sorcha were promptly led out. Agnes realized she had finished her wine again.

"I say." Mr. Hansen, who had been promised Sorcha's second set, cleared his throat. "Miss James? Would you care to dance?" His eyes kept flitting toward Sorcha.

Agnes contemplated her empty glass, then gave a philosophical shrug. "It would be my pleasure, sir."

She enjoyed the rollicking country dance, even though Mr. Hansen's conversation was desultory queries about her family and the weather. He barely finished the figure before charging off to join Sorcha.

But someone else soon asked her to dance. By now the wine had hit her, and she felt giddy and very merry as they went through the figure. When it was over, Agnes found herself, breathless but happy, at the opposite end of the room from where she'd started. Her partner, Lieutenant Murray, brought her a glass of punch and she took a grateful sip, surprised to taste rum. No wonder the Assembly Rooms were so popular.

"She's your sister, is she not?" asked the lieutenant.

Agnes glanced at him. His admiring gaze was on Winnie, who did look beautiful tonight in a cream dress, her red-gold hair in perfect curls. "Yes."

"I say," he began, "you're a splendid girl. Would it be too forward to beg an introduction? I've been watching her all evening, and…" He trailed off sheepishly as Agnes lowered her punch.

"Lieutenant," she asked, "did you ask me to dance to secure an introduction to my sister?"

"No," he protested. "You're jolly fun to talk to."

Jolly fun. Agnes sighed. "How did you know she was my sister?"

Now color rose in his cheeks. "Hansen told me."

That dented her pride. "If you wish, sir."

He beamed at her and resumed watching Winnie with a glazed, happy expression. When the dance ended, Agnes led him over and made the presentation. Her smile grew fixed as Winnie's face grew bright with interest, and took the lieutenant's arm as soon as he asked her to dance.

And then she stood by herself and watched them join the set, the lieutenant's face lit with an animation that hadn't been there during her dance with him.

She sipped the punch, barely noticing the warmth of the rum. Her first visit to the Assembly Rooms, and here she was, stranded alone at the side of the room. Agnes knew she wasn't rich like Ilsa, a beauty like Winnie, or vivacious like Bella. Was it her age?

Her gaze snagged on Sorcha, who was a year older. Sorcha's partner looked as though he might fall to his knees and propose marriage right there in the midst of the dance.

It must be her face. Or perhaps her demeanor.

Rebelliously Agnes gulped down the rest of her punch. She was here, she might as well see the famed rooms. Leaving the glass on a table, she set off to explore.

She reached the saloon between the staircases, where they had come in, without seeing anyone she knew. Every space was crowded and overheated, and she began to feel disenchanted with the place.

"Miss St. James," exclaimed a familiar voice. "Good evening."

"Oh, Mr. Duncan!" Relief surged through her. "How *splendid* to see you!"

He looked happily surprised at this effusive greeting. "The pleasure is mine. I hoped to see you here tonight."

Happiness bubbled up inside her. He was uncommonly attractive in evening clothes, and completely interested in her alone. "Here I am, at long last," she replied gaily. "And the rooms are every bit as magnificent as you said."

He laughed. "I'm delighted to be a reliable source. But it's very crowded tonight! Last week it was easier to talk."

Of course; he must have a subscription, and come regularly.

"Then perhaps we should dance," she said, astonishing herself as much as him.

"We should indeed. But first—" He had a flask, hidden beneath his jacket. "A friend has just become a father," he confided. "We meant to—er—toast his new son."

"How wonderful!" she exclaimed. "May I also congratulate him?" The wine had made her as bold as Sorcha.

"Aye, by all means." He offered his arm and Agnes took it.

The crowd pressed them together as they made their way back into the ballroom. Agnes found she didn't mind, and when one large fellow jostled her rudely, Mr. Duncan growled and put his arm protectively around her.

She didn't mind that *at all*.

He led the way toward a few gentlemen clustered in a

back corner. Agnes sized them up: well-dressed gentlemen about her brother's age. It was perfectly acceptable, she told herself. She stole another glance at Mr. Duncan's firm jaw and broad shoulders. *Very* acceptable.

At their approach, one turned and hailed Mr. Duncan. "There he is! Bring the naftie, man." He flushed as he spotted Agnes. "I beg pardon, miss."

"May I present Messieurs Crawford, Ferrior, Hunter, Gillespie, and MacDougal. Gentlemen, this is Miss St. James," announced Mr. Duncan, pouring whisky into the glasses they discreetly produced. "Her brother is a captain in the army and an old schoolmate of mine, so mind your manners."

Mr. Hunter bowed. She recognized him from the coffeehouse. "A pleasure to make your acquaintance, ma'am."

"Thank you, sir." She smiled. "I understand there is a celebration."

"Aye, Gillespie's son." Another fellow beamed in proud acknowledgement as the men beside him pounded his shoulders.

"To fatherhood!" said someone, and they all drank.

"My warmest felicitations to you and Mrs. Gillespie," Agnes told him.

"Thank 'ee, miss." He put out his glass, and Agnes realized this was far from their first round of toasts, as Mr. Duncan obligingly refilled the glasses.

On impulse, because she was still feeling bold from the wine and because it felt daring but also safe to stand in a secluded corner with these gentlemen—including one of her brother's friends—Agnes asked, "May I?"

Mr. Duncan glanced at her in surprise. "Aye," said Mr. Crawford. He produced another glass and Mr. Duncan tipped his flask over it.

"To Gillespie," said MacDougal. "Not that he did any hard work birthing the babe." Everyone laughed as Gillespie shook his head like a wet dog.

Agnes tossed back the dram with the rest of them. It made her throat burn and her eyes water, but tonight she loved it. She'd had whisky before; it was her mother's standard treatment for monthly female aches.

"To the babe," declared someone. "May he inherit his mother's handsome looks."

"Aye." Mr. Gillespie was visibly, happily drunk. "Poor lad if he takes after me."

Mr. Hunter poured this round. Agnes held out her glass with everyone else. Mr. Duncan shot a look at her, but said nothing.

"To Mrs. Gillespie," declared Agnes, feeling very gregarious now. "The true heroine of this tale."

"Hear, hear!" cried Crawford. "A double toast to her! She married Gill, after all, she's earned it!"

"Aye, she has." The new father hiccuped. "And the dog. He wouldna—he wouldn't leave Betsy's side the whole long while she labored, d' y' know that? 'Tis a damned good dog," slurred Gillespie, now leaning on the man next to him.

"There's no finer companion than a loyal dog," agreed Agnes.

"To the dog!" declared Mr. Ferrior—Agnes thought she had leaned all their names by now. She held out her glass. Mr. Ferrior hesitated, but Agnes gave him a saucy wink, and he poured.

"And to Miss St. James," proposed Mr. Hunter with a gallant flourish. "A most charming young lady."

She smiled and curtsied, but somehow lost her balance and ended up clinging to Mr. Duncan's arm as the gentlemen chuckled and raised their glasses.

"Will you give me that dance now?" murmured Mr. Duncan in her ear.

She gave him a wide smile and tossed back her whisky. "Of course!" She thought she could fly right now, let alone dance. A little bit of whisky was bracing stuff, but it got better and better the more one drank.

He guided her away. Agnes leaned on his arm. Goodness, he was tall and strong. And remarkably handsome. What a brilliant night this was becoming.

"Here." He opened a door behind the gentlemen still toasting the Gillespie birth. "Take a moment to catch your breath."

It was a small chamber, dim and cool and quiet when the door closed behind them. Agnes exhaled in relief, realizing how loud and stuffy the ballroom was. "What is this?"

He looked around. "I think it's a passage to the supper room—or will be, when the room is finished."

There was another door opposite them. Agnes walked over and tried it.

"Let's try the second ballroom," he said. "It's always less crowded."

Agnes wasn't listening. "Oh," she breathed, walking into the unfinished supper room. The walls were still unpainted and ladders stood around the room. The only light came from the tall, bare windows opposite them, lending a ghostly moonlit glow to the furnishings waiting in neat ranks at the side of the room.

She spun around, arms out wide. This wasn't like her—she knew it, somewhere in her tipsy brain—but it did feel glorious. "We shall be the first to dance in here!" Her voice echoed off the walls.

"Shall we?" He followed, watching her warmly.

Agnes stopped whirling, clutching a ladder for balance. His attention was focused on her. He admired *her*. Slowly, a bit unsteadily, she went up to him.

"Would you mind that?" She tipped her head back to see him. "Or do you want to go to the other room and squeeze in amongst the crowd?"

His blue gaze skimmed her face. "Perhaps…not yet."

"No?" She poked him in the chest, then again. She flattened her palm against him, marveling at how solid he was. "Why not?"

His chest expanded under her hand. "We undoubtedly should," he said in a low voice that sent tingles down her spine.

And over her skin.

And made her nipples stand up hard under her stays.

He was so handsome. She plucked a button on his coat. "Do you want to?"

He swallowed. "Want to?"

Agnes fought off a silent fit of giggles. "Dance. In here."

"*Oh.* Aye, I do." He caught her hand and took a formal step away. Another giggle shook Agnes, but she followed his lead and straightened her spine. Competing strains of music from the ballrooms filtered into the room, but they made it through the first few steps. At the places where other dancers would take their turns, Mr. Duncan waved his hands in the air like an energetic musical conductor, making her laugh again. She almost tripped as they clasped hands and skipped down the imaginary row. By the time they should have cast off, she couldn't stop giggling and forgot entirely which way to go, and turned away instead of toward him.

He laughed. Agnes realized her mistake and hastily swung around, only to collide head-on with him. With a startled inhalation he caught her, and Agnes, breathless and exhilarated, flung her arms around him.

"Steady," he said. "I've got you."

He did. Held close to his chest, she felt sheltered, protected, safe. She closed her eyes and pressed closer.

Tentatively his hands moved on her back. His breath warmed her temple. "'Tis glad I am to see you tonight."

Something hot and effervescent shot through her. He wasn't asking to meet her sisters, or passing the time until Sorcha would dance with him. He came to the coffeehouse to see *her*, and talk to *her*. And the expression in his eyes made her feel beautiful and daring, bold and confident, nothing at all like the practical, responsible girl she was supposed to be.

"I'm pleased to see you, too," she whispered, letting her head fall back so she could see his face. "Are you going to kiss me?"

He stopped breathing. His gaze settled on her mouth with an intensity that made her heart flutter. When his head dipped and his arms tightened, she all but jumped to meet him.

The result was a more physical and passionate kiss than either intended, but neither he nor she retreated. Instead Agnes wound her arms around his neck and kissed him back deeply and hungrily.

"My God," he rasped, pressing more kisses down her neck. "*Agnes…*"

She arched her neck in blatant encouragement. Mindlessly she pulled his copper hair free of the tie holding it, plowing her fingers into the crisp waves. A shudder went through his shoulders.

"You're so beautiful," he breathed. "Clever and bold and splendid."

A wild thrill shot through her. Winnie was the beauty, Bella the adventurous one. "Really?" She gave a long shivery sigh as his mouth touched her collarbone, right at the curve between neck and shoulder.

He rested his forehead against hers. "I spend half my life lurking in Agnew's coffeehouse, hoping you'll appear."

An astonished but delighted smile curved her lips. She slid one hand up his chest to tug the end of his neckcloth. "Do you, now?"

He grinned like a guilty boy caught in a secret. "Did you not notice? We've even spoken there, a few times…"

A startled giggle choked her. Somehow her hands had got beneath his coat, wandering over his shoulders. "Aye, I noticed. How could I not, when you bring me plates of soft, warm buns, crying out for a dab of butter? Just seeing you makes me hungry…"

His smile fled. He stared at her, his eyes burning bright. "Aye," he said thickly. "I know the feeling."

He kissed her again, more forcefully this time, his tongue in her mouth and his hand cupping her head. And Agnes thrilled to it.

She spread her hands on his back. He was so big, so warm, so strong… she couldn't stop touching him. The slide of his tongue, hot and possessive, made her stomach flutter and her knees give way. When she almost fell, he cursed even as he laughed, and swept her up in his arms—stumbling into the ladder with another curse, louder this time, making her giggle and kiss his ear, only to get distracted by the smell of his jaw and somehow, inexplicably, bite him there.

"Christ," he gasped, staggering. "Stop!"

"Stop?" She had her arms around his neck, nuzzling the whole side of his face. He smelled so good. Did all men smell this good? Surely not.

"Just for a moment…" He turned and fell backward, landing on one of the sofas with her across his lap. Agnes laughed, clinging to him, and this time his mouth landed on her bosom.

She went still, panting, as his tongue traced delicately along the edge of her bodice, and when his big hand reverently smoothed up her chest to cover her breast, she inhaled so hard it was a miracle she didn't pass out.

It was a fairy tale come to life. This handsome, charming, wonderful man—her brother's friend, whom her papa called a good lad—was holding *her*, looking at her with unconcealed desire, touching her, kissing her, making her burn with wanting.

"Do you like this?" he whispered, his gaze fixed on her

bosom. Agnes watched his fingers, foreign and yet very welcome, feather reverently along the swell of her breast.

"Yes," she said. "*Yes*."

His palm settled over her breast and his thumb stroked her skin. Her breath stopped as she watched his hand, transfixed, feeling as if the world stopped turning as his thumb gently tugged down her bodice.

"Oh…" She couldn't speak as he turned, letting her slip from his arm until she lay against the elegantly curving arm of the sofa, her legs still draped over his. He twisted too, looming over her and lowering his mouth to her bosom again.

Agnes threw back her head and gripped his shoulders; now she *was* flying. His tongue was so soft, so hot. Goosebumps rippled across her skin and she had the wild thought that it would feel so good if he licked her everywhere.

"Felix," she sighed, gripping his head to her.

"Say it again, love," he murmured, easing down the front of her dress. The scooped neckline gave way easily under his touch. And then his hand—so big, so *warm*—cupped her entire breast and his mouth closed on her nipple, and Agnes drew up her knees at the exquisite sensation.

He lavished attention on both her breasts until she was writhing in agony. "Oh, don't stop," she gasped, when he did. "Why did you stop?"

He looked down at her. In the moonlight he was silver and gold, his hair in waves about his taut face. He looked wild and hungry for her. "Ye could drive a man mad," he growled before kissing her again, hard, driving his tongue into her mouth. He tasted of whisky, and the flavor revived her own taste for the spirit. She kissed him back, mimicking what he did to her, biting his lower lip and sucking on his tongue until he shuddered above her.

She clutched at him, desperate for something. Her slipper fell off and hit the floor as she tried to wind herself around him in search of…something. He put his hand on her knee, then almost jerkily flipped up the hem of her dress. Agnes moaned at the heat of his palm on her stockinged calf.

"Christ," he whispered, his voice shaking. "No dream ever compared to this…"

His hand was on her thigh, at her garter. "Do you dream of me?" she managed to gasp in astonishment.

His laugh came out in a strangled huff. "Every bloody night." Another searing kiss as his fingers stroked wickedly up her leg, now between her thighs, now fitting the heel of his hand against her where she ached. His kiss soothed her when she flinched, and then she moaned again and her legs fell open as he touched her, *there*, and she almost died.

"Agnes, love," he breathed in her ear, his cheek against hers as his fingers teased her. "This must be a dream… I'm out of my head, ain't I…"

It had to be a dream. It surpassed anything she'd ever imagined or hoped for. He *dreamt* of her. She moved on instinct to meet his touch. "No… it's too good…"

"Aye." He captured her nipple in his mouth again, and Agnes clung to him with arms and legs as the pleasure he was giving rolled over her like the waves coming into the shore. She was burning—glowing—about to burst into flames—

And it broke her. She gave a gasp, as if she'd nearly drowned, and then another as he slid his fingers *inside* her and the waves of pleasure crashed over her again at the sweet fullness.

For a long moment she shuddered in dazed aftershocks, still clinging to him. He was half under, half over her, his hand between her legs and his head resting on her bosom. His breath was warm and rapid against her skin, almost as frantic as the thud of her heart.

Slowly she opened her eyes. The bare windows glowed with moonlight; the faint sound of music from the ballroom seeped into the room, soft and dreamlike. *She* felt dreamy and soft, as if she were lying on a cloud. Mr. Duncan growled and nestled her more snugly in his arms, kissing her throat, and she almost melted from the pleasure of it.

Idly her fingers combed through his hair. It was long and wavy, and he growled deep in his throat. That made her smile —not that she wasn't already smiling—and when he raised his head to look at her, she put her hands on his face and kissed him.

When she broke the kiss, they stared at each other for a moment. He looked wicked, debauched and beautiful. His coat was askew, his hair was tousled, and his kilt had ridden up his legs. Agnes felt another wave of butterflies inside her as she recognized how aroused he was, sprawled beneath her, looking at her with that blue-flame gaze.

This *was* a fairy tales. Fairies had cast a spell on her, making her beautiful and alluring for one evening of passion. It made her smile, and she kissed him once more.

"I've lost my shoe," she whispered. He blinked, which made her see how ridiculous her words were, and another lunatic giggle overcame her. She leaned over to peer under the sofa but ended up falling on the floor.

"Agnes! Saints, are you hurt?"

She waved aside his exclamation. "No. Where is it?" After a moment's search she dragged it from beneath the sofa, and Felix slipped it back on her foot very gallantly.

He helped her to her feet, and she almost fell right back down. "Easy now," he said as he put an arm around her waist and held her close.

"Don't laugh at me," she said indignantly. "You drank as much as I did!"

"Aye, more." He looked rueful. "We'll both have sore heads tomorrow…"

"I suspect we will," she said gravely, then ruined it with another stifled giggle.

"You…" He trailed off, his gaze moving over her. "You should go back," he finished, his voice thick.

Of course. Her mother would look for her. Oh goodness, what would Mama say if she saw Agnes like this, more than a little tipsy, disheveled from Felix's kisses, and glowing with satisfaction at all of it? It would not be good, she acknowledged. Which was wrong, because she felt absolutely superb. "I should," she agreed. Clumsily she began putting herself back in order. "Are you coming, too?"

He made a vague motion. "Not yet."

She nodded and took a few steps before she had to grab the ladder for support. The floor seemed to be heaving gently beneath her feet, like the deck of a ship.

Not that she'd ever been on a ship.

A thought which made her want to giggle again.

"Agnes," he called.

She looked back at him. Still rumpled and gorgeous, still watching her intently.

"I hope to see you again, very soon."

A silly smile broke out on her face. "Aye. Good night… Felix."

He gave a crooked grin. "Au revoir, Agnes. *Ma chérie*."

Chapter Three

He was going to hell.

What's more, he deserved to go to hell, and burn there for eternity, tormented by every devil in the place.

Felix Duncan lay perfectly still, desperately hoping the images bursting like lightning flashes against the insides of his eyelids were remnants of dreams and fantasies other than proof of the sin he'd committed the night before.

Agnes St. James, head thrown back to bare her beautiful throat all the way down to her glorious breasts.

The pink of her nipple, glistening wet from his tongue.

The feel of her stockinged legs around his waist.

The taste of her mouth, hot and yielding and whisky-flavored.

The sound of her voice, giggling and flirting, breathless and tipsy, urgent and lustful.

The soft, slippery, tight grip of her body around his fingers.

Sweat broke out on his brow—all over his body. Jesus, Mary, and Joseph. Had he really? Had he really been so incredibly, breathtakingly, criminally *stupid*? Had he seduced a young woman, the sister of one of his oldest friends? He said a fervent prayer of thanks that he'd stopped short of actual consummation.

Not that it would pardon what he *had* done.

Which he could not fully remember.

A tap at the door interrupted his despair. "Good morning, sir," called Callum, his manservant. "Are you wanting to rise yet?"

No, he rather thought he would prefer to stay in bed forever. Then he wondered what Agnes must be thinking this morning, and flung himself out of bed with a violence that made his head spin like a top and his stomach revolt. It was only thanks to Callum's quick reflexes that he retched into the chamberpot and not all over the carpet.

"Thank you," he panted several minutes later, sprawled on the floor, one arm around the pot. Callum handed him a steaming cloth, which Felix slapped over his face.

"A hard night, sir?" Callum sounded sympathetic as he moved about the room. There was the splash of water being poured into the basin, then the scrape of the razor against the strop.

"Aye," croaked Felix.

"I feared as much. You looked in a bad way when you came home."

Felix lay still, feeling somewhat better with his face covered by the hot towel. "How so?" He had no memory of reaching his lodgings last night, yet here he was.

"Soused," said his man. "Raving about a marvelous night and pleasures unimaginable one minute, then lapsing into dire melancholy the next. You said you'd been wicked, deserved to be shot, then smiled and said it was all worth it. I didn't know what to make of it."

Perhaps Callum would just draw the razor across his throat. That would solve the matter, thought Felix bleakly.

He propped himself up against the bedpost and tried to think. His brain felt fogged, but he managed to reach one firm conclusion: he had to do something. He'd had his hands between her legs, her breast in his mouth.

For a moment his mind lingered on that, the most glorious moment of his life. By God she was beautiful, even before he saw her breasts in moonlight. And playful; his mouth curved at the thought of their haphazard dance. He remembered laughing as he swung her in his arms, feeling positively buoyant with joy.

But after that sort of intimacy, she would expect something from him. She *deserved* something from him.

He hauled himself to his feet with the aid of the bedpost and staggered to the basin. "I have to go out," he said, and plunged his face into the water.

An hour later, shaved, washed, and dressed, though only marginally steadier on his feet, he reached Parliament Square. The clerk, Mr. Mathison, bowed. "Good morning, Mr. Duncan."

"Good morning, Mathison." He cocked his head questioningly toward the office door.

Thankfully, the clerk nodded. "He is free at present, sir."

With a sigh of relief, Felix let himself in.

Lachlan Duncan barely glanced up from the thick tome spread open in front of him. "A bit early to see the likes of you," he said by way of greeting.

Felix lowered himself gingerly into a chair. "And a good morning to you, Da."

His father eyed him. "It appears to be treating you harshly."

He swallowed. "I've...done something."

His father's brow quirked. "Are the sheriff's officers at your heels?"

"Not that sort of something." He was sweating again, but he resisted the urge to blot his face.

"Don't say you're fighting a duel."

"Not that I know of." Although he might be, if Andrew St. James found out what he had done.

"Ah." His father pushed aside the book. "Then what is it?"

"It involves," he began carefully, "a lady."

Lachlan's eyes narrowed suspiciously. "Is it Miss Hill?"

This was the part Felix was dreading. Catriona Hill was the daughter of Lord Lindow, one of his father's closest friends and colleagues, and Lachlan had been hinting for a few months now that she would make a very suitable wife.

He was probably correct. Catriona was attractive and amiable, with sense and humor. Felix had known her most of his life, and they got on well together. She had a large dowry and impressive connections—unlike Agnes St. James.

But he'd never had the urge to bring Catriona fresh currant buns, or kiss her senseless, or lose his mind and make love to her on a sofa—

"No." A bead of perspiration ran down his temple and he swiped it away.

"And why not? She's a very sensible choice."

"This has naught to do with Miss Hill."

His father leaned back in his chair. "A shame, that," he said grimly. "How bad is it?"

"I… I don't… precisely know." His hands curled into fists on the chair arms. "But what I remember is bad enough."

"Bloody hell, lad," his father growled, running one hand over his close-cropped head. His peruke stood on the stand behind him, the only hair Lachlan wore these days. "You've got to pull yourself about. Getting pickled at the Assembly Rooms is unbecoming."

"How do you know?" He started upright in astonishment. "How do you *know* where I was last night?"

"People tell me things," retorted his father. "I only listen, aye?" He leaned forward. "*How bad?*"

Felix rubbed his forehead, abandoning the fight. He must

have drunk far more than he remembered. He'd never felt this dreadful after a night out. "I need to make a... a proposal of marriage."

"Christ!" Lachlan erupted out of his seat. "What were you thinking?"

Obviously I was not, Felix replied, but only inside his aching head. "As you say, I was...a trifle tipsy." *Drunk as a wheelbarrow.* "In my every memory, she was willing, but she's a respectable lady."

His father grunted. "Please say she's a widow."

Felix scowled at the peruke on the faceless head and said nothing.

"What the bloody hell were you thinking?" snapped his father again.

"We were drinking whisky—both of us—and things... happened."

"Well, perhaps not enough!" Lachlan exclaimed. "Did she demand any promises?"

Felix knew better than to think that mattered.

Lachlan sighed at his silence. "Before you do anything irrevocable, make certain that you must. It's a bad way to start a marriage. You'll have to see this lass every day at your breakfast table." He paused, eyeing Felix with a frown. "Better yet, wait a day. Go home and sleep it off, and see how things stand tomorrow. You look pitiable."

I feel pitiable. "If I must, I should do it at once," he argued, imagining once again what Agnes must be thinking and feeling.

His father shook his head, looking furious, then paused. "Perhaps she'll say no."

His head felt stuffed with wool. "If it pleases you to hope so," he mumbled.

Lachlan grunted and resumed his seat. He pulled the law book toward him again and bent over it in dismissal. "Nothing about this pleases me. Notify me of her answer."

"I will."

He left his father's chambers and headed for the coffee-house, hoping to settle his stomach and steady his brain. William Hunter was in disgustingly good spirits when Felix collapsed into the chair across from him. "Looking haggard today," he said, watching over the wire rims of his spectacles.

Felix raised one hand and Helen came over. "Coffee," he begged. "Scalding hot and as strong as the devil."

Hunter's shoulders shook with laughter as he made a note on the brief before him. "*Feeling* haggard as well, I see."

Felix propped his elbows on the table and put his face in his palms. "Wheest, man."

His partner laughed harder.

He lifted his head. "Do you recall the young woman last night, toasting Gillespie with us?"

Hunter's brows went up and he glanced toward the table by the window where Agnes and Mrs. Ramsay usually sat. "I do indeed. The pretty girl you flirt with here."

Oh God. He'd forgotten about that, his very public atten-tions to Agnes. "Have you heard anything about her today?"

Hunter snorted, turning back to the brief. "No, why?"

Right. Hunter had no wife, no sister, just an older lady who kept his rooms and read her Bible when she wasn't cleaning. "I shouldn't have let her join us," he murmured to himself. Even if it *had* been a thrill to see Agnes toss back her whisky.

Good lord, was that why she'd kissed him? Surely not; the drams had been small, and she'd only had two. Maybe three. That wasn't enough to make a lady drunk, was it?

"No, likely not," said Hunter. "More to the point, how did your lovemaking succeed?"

Felix stared blankly.

"When you left us," prompted his friend. "No one saw you for an age."

His heart froze. "What?" he croaked.

Hunter peered over his spectacles again. "Did you summon the nerve to kiss the lass?"

God save him. It felt like there was an anvil atop his chest.

"Will her brother thrash you?" Hunter changed tacks when Felix just stared at him, speechless with horror.

He was sweating profusely now, and his eyes burned. Andrew St. James would indeed thrash him—if not for the whisky, certainly for what came after it. He had to make things right with Agnes before her brother returned to Edinburgh.

A smirking Helen brought his coffee, fiercely hot and strong. Felix burned his tongue on the first sip but drained the cup anyway.

"Have you spoken to MacDonald about this?" Hunter pushed the brief in front of him and tapped one paragraph. "It's a reach, in my opinion."

The words were mere wavy lines on the paper. People had noticed him leaving with Agnes. Who gave a bloody damn what the brief said? "No," he managed to say, lurching to his feet. "I've got an appointment—your pardon—"

He barely made it to the alley before throwing up against a brick wall.

Chapter Four

I know how to enjoy myself and not get into trouble.

Agnes curled into a tight ball under the covers. Her head ached and she knew she deserved it.

Outside the door her sisters were arguing over the mirror. They shared the largest room, across the corridor, and their mother had the narrow room in the middle. Agnes was fortunate to have a room to herself, even if it was so small she could touch both walls if she stretched out her arms. But today, of all days, she would have been grateful to have a broom cupboard to hide in, just for the privacy.

Bad: she had let Felix Duncan make love to her last night.

Worse: she had encouraged him. *Begged* him.

Worst of all: she'd found it intoxicating and thrilling and wanted more.

It was entirely normal to find a gentleman handsome and charming. It was even acceptable to flirt with him in the coffeehouse and dance with him at the Assembly Rooms.

It was quite another thing—and unpardonably wicked—to kiss him, and ask him to kiss her back, and let him untie her bodice and kiss her breasts. She dimly remembered putting her legs around him, which was scandalous, and she definitely remembered the keen pleasure he gave her when he put his hand between her legs, which was sinful beyond belief.

What a lark, she'd thought; a dram of whisky. Two drams. Maybe three. She drank whisky—not often, and not in quantity, but she could hold her liquor. She'd thought.

Of course, that was on top of two glasses of wine.

And the horrid rum punch.

She covered her head and moaned.

"Agnes?"

She started violently and whipped the blanket down to see her mother in the doorway.

"Are you well?" Mama stepped in, her face concerned.

"Yes of course," Agnes blurted, then realized she was not. "I—I have a stomachache."

Her mother's face softened in sympathy, driving a spike of guilt through Agnes's heart. "Of course. You looked unwell on the way home last night. Stay in bed and rest. Winnie and Bella can help me in the shop enough for one day. Would you like a dram of—?"

"No!" Flushed and miserable, Agnes shook her head. "Perhaps a hot brick." Her stomach did hurt, and she could bang the brick against her head.

"Of course. I'll tell Annag to bring one before I go."

To the shop. Where someone might march in and tell her that Agnes had been drinking last night, with gentlemen, and then had disappeared with a man.

"Mama!" She sat up in bed hastily, and her head felt like it might pop right off her neck and burst against the wall, like a soap bubble. "I need to return Mrs. Ramsay's magazine. May I take it back to her?"

Her mother paused.

"I promised I would bring it today," Agnes added hastily. "I won't stay." She had to discover what, if anything, people were saying about her. Agnes barely remembered coming home last night, let alone what she'd done after leaving Felix. But Ilsa would know, and Ilsa would tell her.

"All right," said her mother, and Agnes tried to find the magazine.

They often met in the morning and read the latest lady's magazines from London together. Mama couldn't afford them, but Ilsa took several and Agnes studied each one for helpful ideas for the shop. Normally it was good fun, a small respite from working, a chance to see her friend.

Today Agnes kept her face down as she hurried to Ilsa's house. She was sure the marks of sin were branded on her skin for the world to see.

Ilsa lived in one of the large old houses in the High Street, fortunately only a short distance from the narrow close where the St. James's more modest lodgings stood. Agnes intercepted Ilsa on her front step, just setting out. "Good morning," she said breathlessly. "I'm not feeling well today."

Ilsa touched her arm in concern.

Agnes waved one hand. "Nothing serious. But…" She lowered her voice further. "Last night…"

A smile crossed her friend's face. "Yes? Was he charming?"

Her heart froze. "What?"

"The handsome attorney who brings us currant buns." Ilsa's brow wrinkled in confusion. "I saw you speaking with him last night… No. I see he is not whom you wish to discuss."

Her face burned. "No. Yes. What—Last night. I did speak with him." Ilsa waited, perplexed. Agnes gulped for air. "And I walked out with him."

Now Ilsa looked wildly curious. "What happened? Was he rude or impertinent?"

It was impossible to be more humiliated than she was at this moment. "We only took a brief stroll. But I'm worried— what people might say—"

"Hush." Ilsa took her hand. "I heard no one speak of it last night. I didn't see you again after that. I presumed you had gone home! It was late."

She calmed a little. "Yes. I did go home." Too late, as it turned out. "I had too much… punch and wondered if I made a spectacle of myself."

Ilsa smiled. "No! If you had, I would have rushed to your side—not to stop you, of course, but to join you."

Agnes laughed, as Ilsa had intended, and it was only half tragic. She bade her friend farewell and went home, relieved that her mother and sisters had left by the time she returned. Annag came to fuss over her, bringing a hot brick wrapped in a flannel and a cup of chamomile tea, and Agnes retreated to her bed.

Perhaps she was worried over nothing. Perhaps no one had seen her drinking whisky, or leaving with Felix Duncan, or noted how long she was gone. It was her very first time attending the Assembly Rooms; perhaps no one had even noticed her.

But it was better to be prepared. If asked about it, what could she say?

She could admit that she spoke to Mr. Duncan; such a dear old friend of Drew's. If asked, she would admit to drinking more wine that she ought, with deepest penitence and heart-felt promises never ever to do so again. If pressed, she would admit to stepping out with Mr. Duncan for a breath of fresh air. If absolutely, unavoidably necessary, she would admit to exploring the still-unfinished supper room, purely out of idle curiosity, and confess that oh yes, *now that you mention it*, Mr. Duncan had accompanied her.

She would never, ever admit to kissing him, nor to throwing herself at him, and most especially not to encouraging him to take the most shocking and indecent liberties.

Yes, don't stop. Why did you stop?

She huddled under the blanket, feeling again the delicate

stroke of his fingers on her cheek, the hunger in his kiss, the effortless way he swung her into his arms. Heat flushed through her at the thought of how he'd looked at her in the moonlight, and how he'd made her laugh. Her breath grew short at the memory of his low, rough whispers against her skin: *Agnes, my love…*

Oh, it had been so wickedly *wonderful*.

He said he hoped to see her again soon. What would she say to him? Would she spontaneously combust on the spot, in a mixture of awkwardness and desire?

Annag tapped at her door. "There's a gentleman here," she said in disapproval. "Insists on seeing you."

Her throat closed up. "Who is it?"

Lips pursed, Annag gave her the card. Felix Duncan. Agnes's heart leapt even as her stomach knotted in alarm.

It was too early for a formal call. What did he want? And she shouldn't receive a gentleman alone anyway. It was safer to send him away.

Then she pictured him returning when her mother was home and curious, and lurched out of bed. "Oh," she said over the pounding of her pulse. "He's an old friend of Drew's. I'll be down soon."

At Drew's name, Annag's face brightened. She'd been his nurse when he was a child and all three girls agreed that she loved him best. "Aye," she said more happily, and went out.

Remain calm, Agnes commanded herself, staring at her pale reflection in the mirror. *Don't panic.*

After all, perhaps he'd come for a good reason. Hadn't she hoped he might call? Some of her anxiety faded. Yes, they'd been indiscreet, and a wee bit drunk, but she also remembered him saying he dreamt about her. Warmth filled her. He'd called her beautiful, and held her tenderly, and kissed her so hungrily…

Perhaps he'd come to make certain she was well. Perhaps he'd laugh with her a little more in that warm, teasing way he had, perhaps even confide that it *had* gone too far the previous evening, but he couldn't regret it because he'd been nursing a tendre for her and would like to call on her, court her, see if they suited each other when not tipsy on whisky…

Perhaps there was no reason for alarm. Perhaps there was a happy-ever-after ending to this.

She smoothed her hair, pinched her cheeks, and hurried down the stairs.

He rose at her entrance. Agnes paused, startled. His face was dead white, his eyes red-rimmed. He faced her, his mouth pinched, then bowed stiffly. If ever a man looked like he was walking toward death, Felix Duncan did.

"Good morning, sir." She curtsied, ducking her head to hide her resurgent flare of panic. "Pray sit down." She took her own seat.

He sank slowly onto the edge of the sofa, as if the action pained him. "I hope you are well today, Miss St. James."

Oh dear. Not an encouraging beginning. Unable to meet his eyes, she pulled at a loose thread in the hem of her apron. "Yes, thank you."

He took a deep breath. "I offer my unreserved apologies for last night." He cleared his throat. "For coercing you to drink the whisky."

She remembered asking for that whisky. "That was not your fault," she murmured, blushing. "You do not owe me an apology."

"No." He started to shake his head, then hunched his shoulders with a grimace. "No, I most certainly do. I regret every moment deeply."

Oh dear. Worse and *worse*.

"Second…" He swallowed. "I believe I committed actions which compromised your honor and could besmirch your good name. Accordingly, I have come to offer you my own name and hand, if you will do me the honor of becoming my wife."

Her mouth had slowly fallen open through this speech. "What?" was all she could say.

Staring fixedly beyond her ear, he repeated woodenly, "Would you do me the honor of becoming my wife?"

"No—wait—*you believe*—do you not remember?" He had scrambled her wits, apparently.

A dull flush crept up his cheekbones, highlighting the pallor of the rest of his complexion. His face glistened with perspiration. "I know I owe you this."

For the second time that day, Agnes wanted to crawl into bed and stay there. So much for her hope that he'd come out of concern, or even interest. *I owe you this.*

"No, Mr. Duncan," she whispered.

He blinked, then focused his gaze on her for the first time in several minutes. "No? *What?*"

"No," she said again. "No, thank you."

He stared. "But why?"

Anger began to burn away the fog of humiliation. "I do not think we suit each other."

"What? *Bollocks.*" He dropped his head into his hands.

She realized what was the matter then. Mortified and furious, Agnes shot up from her chair. "You're still drunk!"

He raised his head and scowled before rising, slowly and unsteadily. "I am not." He ruined this flat denial by swallowing heavily and swaying on his feet.

How could she have longed for this man to call on her? He looked grim and miserable, resigned to marrying her because he thought he must. All trace of the warmth and admiration he'd displayed in the coffeehouse—and the Assembly Rooms—was gone.

Agnes would sooner cut off her hair and join a pirate crew than enter into such a marriage, even with him.

"I think you'd better go," she choked out.

"You're… you're refusing?"

Her face burned at his shocked tone. "As incomprehensible as that may be to you, I am. That's no sort of marriage, and not one I would ever accept. Please go, sir."

He stared at her, his blue eyes burning. Agnes marched to the door and opened it. "Thank you for coming to call, Mr. Duncan," she said formally, mindful of Annag's eavesdropping presence.

Still he hesitated. "Your answer is no? Truly? You can't mean it. What we did last night—"

She flew across the room and seized his arm. "Get—out!" She pushed him toward the door.

Stumbling over his own feet, he went. Breathing hard, Agnes listened for the door below.

Had that really happened?

Had he actually thought she would accept such a grim proposal?

Had *everything* he said last night been a lie?

Had she really been half in love with him?

Thank God he was gone, and she would…only have to see him all over town, again and again and again, especially when Drew returned and inevitably spoke to his old friend. Ilsa had teased her about inviting him to tea and golf.

With a moan of distress, she ran to the window.

From a distance, he was as handsome as ever. The sun shone on his copper hair, curling in a queue at his nape. His shoulders were magnificently broad in his dark green coat, and when he paused to glance upward, she caught a glimpse of his face: piercing blue eyes, narrow nose, sculpted mouth set in a thin line. From up here he didn't look drunk, or callous.

He pulled out a handkerchief and blotted his face—probably in relief, Agnes thought in mortification. He walked slowly away, giving her a good look at his muscled calves. She pressed one hand to her chest, over her hammering heart, and watched him disappear.

Chapter Five

Felix spent the next four days in bed, wracked by fever and nausea.

In more lucid moments, he acknowledged that he ought to have taken his father's advice and not rushed to see Agnes. With his head splitting, his stomach roiling, and the first tremors of fever making his eyes burn, he'd made a thorough and complete shambles of that proposal.

And she'd said no. Not just no, but that she'd never accept him. He had been almost delirious by the time he returned to his lodging, but he remembered that part.

In more feverish hours, he dreamt of her in his arms again, but this time she was saying *no no no* as he kissed her and touched her. And his own voice echoed mockingly back at him: *no? But—why?*

Because you're a damned idiot, he told himself.

It was always a relief to wake from those nightmares and find himself alone in bed, the sweat-soaked sheets twisted around his body.

On the fifth day the fever broke. When Callum asked if he felt like eating, Felix nodded and ventured to try a simple oatcake. He even propped himself up in bed and looked through his messages while waiting to see if the oatcake would stay in his stomach or come right back up, as had everything else he'd eaten since That Night.

His father had sent a note two days ago: *What is the verdict?*

Felix closed his eyes for a moment, then scrawled *Refused* across the bottom and sent Callum to deliver it. That, he knew, was the last his father would say about the subject. Lachlan Duncan would be pleased he had escaped.

He tried not to dwell on it, either. He'd been miserable with fever, trying not to be sick again, but Agnes had said no, definitively and emphatically. He would have to find a new coffeehouse to frequent. Occupy his mind. Teach himself not to look for dark curls and impish blue eyes and a generous smile around every corner.

Hunter complained bitterly when Felix refused to meet him at Agnew's anymore.

"They roast the coffee berries to cinders here," he complained as they sat in Peterson's coffeehouse by the Grassmarket. "And there's no Helen." The woman serving was old enough to be Felix's mother, with a stern manner. She thumped the dishes down in front of them without a word

"Helen deserves a respite from serving you," Felix told him.

Hunter glowered. "Why won't you go to Agnew's? 'Tis damned inconvenient to walk all the way over here."

"It's five minutes' walk."

"Then why not walk those five minutes to Agnew's?" Hunter sipped his coffee with an expression of distaste. "Did you annoy the proprietor and get banned?"

"I prefer it here." Stubbornly he hunched over the brief and marked another change.

"Well, I don't." Hunter pushed back his chair and dropped a coin on the table. "I'm going back. You know where to find me."

Felix grunted as his partner left. He also missed Agnew's, where Helen knew just when to pour fresh coffee and brought gooseberry jam for the buns without being asked. He missed the larger windows that brightened the place, and the more comfortable chairs. He missed being able to catch almost anyone practicing law, coming or going from the courts across the street.

And most of all he missed carrying currant buns to a pair of beautiful ladies and making them smile. Did Agnes still go to Agnew's?

No. He was not going to think of her. She did not want him, and he needed to forget her.

He threw himself into every other pursuit imaginable. He dug out the violin he hadn't played in several years and tuned it up. He started going to the fencing salon again, morbidly telling himself it could be useful preparation for a duel. He took on more new clients in an attempt to keep himself busy and distracted.

It worked, somewhat, until Andrew St. James arrived in town.

St. James had written to ask if he had a spare bed. He would be in Edinburgh for a few weeks and didn't relish staying with his family. At the time, Felix had been flush with optimism about his flirtation with Agnes, and it had seemed a splendid idea to have her brother, his oldest friend, to stay. It might offer all manner of excuses to see her outside the coffeehouse. He'd sent his affirmative reply immediately.

Now, obviously, it was the most idiotic idea he'd ever had.

He prepared himself not to twitch at the sound of her name. He schooled himself to avoid mentioning her. He was still completely unprepared when Drew St. James explained what had brought him back to Edinburgh.

Through some dark miracle, Drew was now heir presumptive to his distant cousin, the Duke of Carlyle. He had letters and documents attesting to it, signed and sealed by the duke's attorney. At some point in the future—and Drew said that it would likely be sooner than later—he would be a duke.

Which meant Agnes would be a lady, the sister of a duke, an heiress. She could expect far more than any humble Edinburgh attorney had to offer.

Had she known? Had she refused him not merely because of his clumsy approach, but because she knew she could do much better than the likes of him?

Not that it mattered. He'd been rejected, either way.

AGNES SPENT the days after Mr. Duncan's disastrous visit—she would not even think of it as a proposal—trying to forget it had ever happened. She needed time to brace herself for the inevitable moment when her brother mentioned him, or even worse, invited him to the house.

Her first brilliant idea was to flee. "Mama," she said to her mother, "Drew will be home any day now, and the house will be quite crowded."

Her mother smiled fondly. "It will, and in the best way!"

"It seems unfair to make Bella sleep on the floor," Agnes went on. That was her mother's plan: to make room for their brother, Agnes would move out of her room into her sisters', where Bella would make up a pallet on the floor. "You wouldn't want her to get a pain in her back from it. And Heaven forbid Winnie or I step on her in the night."

Her mother paused. It was true that Winnie's and Bella's room was cramped even for the two of them.

Cautiously, Agnes added, "Mrs. Ramsay has kindly invited me to stay with her, for everyone's comfort."

She held her breath. Ilsa had indeed invited her, after Agnes dropped a few suggestive comments. Ilsa's home was only a few minutes' walk away. She would barely be gone.

But Mama was not overly fond of Ilsa Ramsay. When

Agnes and she were newly friends, Mama had invited Ilsa to tea one Sunday afternoon. It had not gone well. Ilsa had gone golfing that morning instead of to church. She arrived wearing a beautiful bright pink gown, even though her husband had only been dead for eight months; and she came on her own, without a maid or a chaperone. The St. James girls were deeply impressed by this blithe disregard for gossip and convention, but Mama was not. She sternly told her daughters that such things were tolerable in a widow of good fortune, but not in ladies of their station, and they were not to get any ideas about aping Mrs. Ramsay.

Today, though, the argument about Bella's comfort outweighed that concern. Mama finished her notations in the ledger before looking up. "I would hate for you to impose on Mrs. Ramsay."

"She assured me she would welcome my company," Agnes hastened to say. "And it would only be for a month, aye?"

Drew, as usual, had written only the one letter, scant with details of any kind. But he could hardly stay very long. He would have to return to his regiment.

"A month only," said her mother with visible reluctance.

Agnes beamed in relief and genuine delight. Ilsa's house was much larger and more comfortable, and no one there would scold her about taking too much time at the mirror. "Thank you, Mama!"

She packed a trunk and moved to Ilsa's the next day. She still went to the shop, and she would obviously return home to see her brother, but just this slight distance let her breathe easier.

Ilsa asked only once about the handsome lawyer who used to bring them fresh currant buns and tea, when Agnes suggested they go to a different coffeehouse than Agnew's. "Oh! I'm sure he's off flirting with someone else," Agnes managed to reply lightly. "I've forgotten all about him."

That was a lie. Agnes had to stop herself from looking for him every day in the streets, and then she had to cope with the mingled relief and disappointment when she didn't see him.

She didn't understand herself. Rationally she should never want to see Mr. Duncan again; irrationally she kept hoping for a glimpse of his broad-shouldered figure, his teasing smile. Rationally, it was best for both of them if he kept out of her way; irrationally, she wished they might run into each other and go back to the easy flirtation they had shared before That Night.

There had been no gossip about her disappearance in his company, and she should be on her knees thanking God and all the saints for that. Instead she was tormented by vivid memories of that evening, both waking and sleeping. A man's laugh in the street would sound like his, and start an answering smile on her face, before she remembered. From time to time she had to walk past Agnew's, and the mere scent of currant buns baking would bring back the flush of pleased excitement that he was going to bring them to her table.

How had it all gone so wrong? Perhaps if she had listened to Ilsa and treated him like a real suitor, she wouldn't have lost her mind the first moment she was alone with him. Those memories were the ones she wished desperately to forget: the giddy feeling of being swept up in his arms, the stark awe in his face when he looked at her, the catch in his voice when he breathed *Agnes, love* as his wickedly wonderful fingers stroked her…and most of all, the look he gave her at the end, when he called her darling.

She lay awake at night wondering if she had crossed an invisible boundary that she could never uncross, from respectable young lady to secret wanton. She hoped not. She prayed not. Every day she told herself the longings and urges would go away, along with her incessant feeling that he was just around the next corner, and the small jolt of anxious eagerness that wrought within her.

It was her brother who finally managed to blow away thoughts of Felix Duncan from Agnes's mind. He reached Edinburgh armed with a thunderbolt of news: through the most amazing chain of circumstances, he now stood next in line for their English cousin's dukedom of Carlyle, with a castle in England and hundreds of acres of land all over Britain. The Duchess of Carlyle had given Drew a healthy income and sent expensive gifts for them. And Drew meant for them all to go live near the castle, so he could prepare to assume the title.

Agnes was horrified. Leave Edinburgh—their home, Papa's grave, her shop? It was unthinkable. What would they do in England? None of *them* would inherit anything. Drew would be off learning how to wear a ducal coronet and preside over an enormous estate, while she and her sisters would be... nobodies. They could not even petition to become ladies until their brother inherited, which wouldn't happen until the current duke died. They would be the poor Scottish relations, for heaven only knew how many years, and Agnes wanted none of it.

Drew, oblivious man, inadvertently delivered a coup de grâce trying to portray it positively. "I intend to settle a proper dowry on you," he told her, walking her back to Ilsa's house.

Thank goodness it was dark. Her face burned at that word, *dowry*. A dowry was meant to help a woman elicit a marriage proposal, and she'd already done that. Received it, rejected it, and had to take it to her grave, even though it felt like she might explode from keeping it to herself.

There was literally no one she could tell. Mama would be horrified that she'd been meeting a man at the coffeehouse. Her sisters would find it dashing and romantic and pester her to explain why she'd rejected it. Ilsa would suspect something terrible had happened at the Assembly Rooms, because she'd seen how Agnes flirted with him. And Drew would probably demand answers from his friend, which could lead to a duel or at least a fight.

It was too much. She fled into Ilsa's house, wishing she had never set eyes on Felix Duncan.

Chapter Six

Felix's intention to keep his distance, physically and mentally, from Agnes St. James was taking hits from all sides.

"I saw your lady the other day," said William Hunter.

"What?" His mind was on the case they were to argue. He had agreed to return to Agnew's coffeehouse but only after a certain hour, when Agnes was unlikely to be there. To atone for his absence he drank multiple pots of coffee and left lavish tips for Helen.

"Miss St. James." Hunter tapped the side of his nose.

He flinched and tried to hide it by reaching for his cup. "She's not my lady."

"No? How'd you spoil that, then? I thought you'd got the inside lane, being such friends with her brother."

His mates knew Andrew St. James was staying with him; the pair of them had gone out to an oyster cellar with Adam Monteith and Will Ross for an evening of revelry. Thankfully, they knew nothing else.

"If you think being friends with her brother is the way to a lass's heart," he replied, "I see why you're still unwed."

Hunter laughed, but let it go.

St. James, on the other hand, presented greater difficulties. Not only was he staying in Felix's own home, he'd become infatuated with Ilsa Ramsay. She had been at the oyster cellar, and had danced with St. James.

Felix had watched his friend steal glances at the beautiful widow all night. He had also scanned the room with wholly inappropriate hope, to see if Agnes might possibly be with Mrs. Ramsay. Which he knew was unlikely, and irrelevant to him anyway, but St. James's open interest was like a stone in his shoe.

When St. James invited him three days later to come along to fetch his sisters from Calton Hill, Felix was on his feet and at the door before he remembered he was keeping his distance. It was a sickness, he told himself, this yearning for any chance to see her. And it went as expected: Agnes turned white, then pink, at the sight of him, and she determinedly ignored him before hurrying away with her sisters. They did not exchange a single word.

St. James was too moon-struck over Mrs. Ramsay to notice. Felix made an excuse and strode home, telling himself it was time to get over her.

But...ah Lord above, she looked so fine in the sunlight with her color high and the wind ruffling the dark wisps of hair at the nape of her neck. He recalled how exquisitely soft her skin was there, that night she'd kissed him and held him close. *Just seeing you makes me hungry...* If only there were some way he could fix things with her...

And then St. James offered him just that. "You didn't tell me you knew her," he charged when he returned from the hill.

Felix gave a guilty start. "Why should I? It's not a crime to know someone."

"You might have mentioned it!"

"There was nothing to tell," he muttered. And never would be. Some things he was taking to his grave.

"Hmph. She specifically named you, idiot, and said I should invite you to visit Stormont Palace with us."

For a moment the angels in heaven seemed to sing. She had spoken of him—invited him somewhere, anywhere, it didn't matter where; *with us*.

His elation died a quick death when he realized his friend thought he'd been flirting with Ilsa Ramsay. His heart, which had soared at the thought of Agnes softening toward him and wanting to invite him on an outing, turned to lead and fell into his boots. He resorted to mocking his friend about his fascination with the beautiful widow, and even suggested he might *start* flirting with her. The words tasted like ashes, but it distracted St. James from any suspicion about Agnes.

God. He was a sad case. He *ought* to start flirting with another woman, if only to save himself from collapsing into melancholy.

Accordingly, that night he went to the Assembly Rooms, determined to make a clean start. He danced with Catriona Hill, who would be an ideal wife, and with Lady Talbot, a flirty widow who would be a willing lover. He drank whisky with James Crawford and Tom MacDougal—not nearly as much as he'd drunk That Night, but just enough to weaken his resolve to stay away when he caught sight of Agnes sitting with Mrs. Ramsay, smiling and laughing.

All thought of Miss Hill and Lady Talbot fled his brain. Agnes was still the woman he wanted, damn it.

What did he have to lose? He made his way through the crowd and swept a bow. "Good evening, Mrs. Ramsay." Her gaze flashed his way, still bright and happy, and the breath caught in his throat. "Miss St. James."

For a split second he had the wild hope she would nod politely, perhaps smile. He could offer to fetch her some wine, even ask her to dance. He could apologize and explain. He could do so much better than last time…

Instead she shot to her feet, snapped, "Good evening, sir,"

and then was gone—but not before he saw the flash of panic in her eyes. Agnes, he realized as he watched her go, was frightened.

This was the same room where their indiscretion had begun. Tonight was much the same as that night, the rooms crowded with dancers, loud and festive with conversation and music. Did she fear he'd come to lure her into another indiscretion?

Would she think that of him? It was a disconcerting possibility.

He turned back to Mrs. Ramsay, who was watching him curiously. "I hoped I might beg the honor of a dance, ma'am."

"Of course." She smiled brightly, as if she too wanted a distraction. From the corner of one eye, Felix caught sight of Andrew St. James swinging Flora Clapperton down the reel and understood; he and Mrs. Ramsay were making good use of each other.

After the dance he lingered by her side and made conversation, wishing he dared ask if Agnes had confided in her. If she had, he doubted Mrs. Ramsay would be so cordial toward him. No, Felix decided, she'd probably not told anyone. Perhaps she feared *he* had?

Mrs. Ramsay's next words scattered those thoughts. "I shall miss them so, when they have all moved house to England with the captain," she said, nodding toward Winifred and her sister Isabella, who were holding court before a handful of captivated young men.

Felix stopped cold. "England! The devil you say!"

Her eyes filled with understanding. "Didn't the captain tell you? He's considering removing there, to be near his future...responsibilities. Winifred and Isabella are enthralled by the prospect of a Season in London as well."

Damn it. "When?"

"I don't know," she said softly. "Perhaps you should ask him, as *his* dear friend."

The whole time they'd been speaking—the whole bloody evening—he'd been aware of Agnes. She was laughing gaily with a pair of soldiers from the Castle—fellows like her brother. He'd caught her looking at him and Mrs. Ramsay, and he'd hoped it would make her the tiniest bit intrigued, perhaps even willing to speak to him again.

But she was leaving Edinburgh, to take her place as sister of a future duke, an eligible lady and heiress. And she'd already rejected him. *Don't forget about that*, said a spiteful voice inside his head.

"Perhaps it doesn't much matter," he muttered.

"I wouldn't be so sure," Mrs. Ramsay replied.

St. James was plowing through the crowd, his expression intent. Felix took a breath and mustered a smile for his companion. "Only time will tell, aye? And as long as *you* don't say you're leaving Edinburgh, I shan't mourn. St. James was gone for years and I never once missed a minute of sleep over it."

She was laughing when St. James reached them, a smile on his lips but his eyes alert. He'd come to ask her to dance, as Felix had expected; wanting to twit his friend, he leapt in with a request of his own, but she refused them both, for she'd already promised the dance to Mr. Grant.

They watched her walk off on the merchant's arm. Felix's mind was still absorbing the news that Agnes would be leaving Edinburgh, eliminating any chance of a rapprochement. He'd told himself his chances were virtually nil, but was just realizing that his heart had still clung to hope. This planned visit to Stormont Palace had appeared to be a shining opportunity to apologize, perhaps begin again. Once she left Edinburgh, though...

"Tell the truth," demanded St. James, eyeing him suspiciously. "Why did you dance with her?"

Felix shrugged. "'Twas just a dance. You were dancing with other women yourself."

St. James flushed. "Friends of my sisters. They introduced me."

Felix made himself smirk. "I'm sure Mrs. Ramsay assumed that very thing, as you led out half a dozen attractive single women of good fortune."

His friend glared, then sighed. "Aye." He gave a nod and walked off. He would have a second chance with Mrs. Ramsay. The sparkle in her eye when she looked at him was plain for all to see. Felix, on the other hand, felt as though his last chance had just been snuffed out.

Now the music was making his head hurt. He turned and headed for the door, no longer in the mood for dancing or flirting.

AGNES WAS GOING QUIETLY MAD.

Everywhere she turned were reminders of Felix Duncan. First, the Assembly Rooms themselves, where she'd been so happy to see him, where his eyes had lit up in admiration and delight at the sight of her. She knew *that* had been real, as real as her own attraction to him.

Then the man himself turned up and began flirting with Ilsa. Agnes knew she didn't hold a candle to her friend in terms of eligibility. Ilsa's father was a town councillor, head of the most powerful tradesmen's guild in the city. The Duncans were an old family of advocates and judges, well-to-do and respected in Edinburgh. Ilsa would be a very good match for Felix, and he for her. It was entirely logical for him to flirt with Ilsa, she told herself.

But she couldn't bear to watch, so she fled as soon as he approached. She was a coward, but she still couldn't face him in person. Too late she realized both her sisters were dancing, and she didn't want to stand by herself like an outcast. She settled for joining Sorcha White, but once again all the gentlemen who clustered around them ignored her for Sorcha.

From there she'd watched in quiet misery as Ilsa danced with Felix, both of them looking tremendously pleased, and then strolled arm in arm, his ginger head bent near her dark one. They made a handsome couple.

"Miss St. James, would you like to dance?" asked a gentleman, puncturing her thoughts.

"Hmm? Ah..." She hesitated. Sorcha was walking off with a lieutenant, and the gentleman's eyes tracked her.

"Did you ask Miss White?" she blurted out.

He nodded, still watching Sorcha. "She's promised me the next set."

Once again, a man was only asking her to dance because he was waiting for the partner he really wanted. And the only man who had ever wanted to dance with *her* was off with Ilsa.

"Thank you, no," she said with a forced smile. "I believe I'm done dancing this evening."

He took it cheerfully, bowing and excusing himself. Alone again, Agnes scanned the room for her brother. Only her second visit to the Assembly Rooms, and now it was ruined, too. Her mother hadn't come tonight, counting on Drew to see his sisters home safely. She wished she *could* go home, but Drew, like Winnie and Bella, was still dancing.

Upon learning of their brother's inheritance, and realizing he would need a wife, Winnie and Bella had begun scheming to find him a Scottish bride, rather than waiting for him to marry an Englishwoman. They had introduced him to every eligible girl in the room and coerced him to dance with all of them. Her brother hadn't missed a single set. Her sisters would probably keep him occupied all night. And when they weren't introducing Drew to young ladies, Winnie and Bella had plenty of dance partners of their own.

Agnes was the only one feeling lost.

Listless, she wandered into the saloon. Tonight the supper

room across the way was open, brilliantly lit, the tall doors opened to admit guests. She turned away from it, not wanting to remember what had happened in there.

Her throat grew tight. *Why* had she drunk so much That Night? Not for the first time she wondered what might have happened if she hadn't asked for whisky, if she'd simply accepted his request to dance. If they'd just talked. Laughed. He might have asked to call on her or escort her home. Tonight she could have been as excited as her sisters to attend the Assembly Rooms, because he would be here, waiting to dance with her again—

As if the gods had heard her, Felix Duncan strode out of the main ballroom directly toward her, his dark green kilt swinging around his legs, his sable jacket perfectly fitted over his broad shoulders. His head was down, so he didn't see her freeze like a startled deer.

He looked up. Like her, he stopped dead in his tracks. For a moment they just stared at each other.

Agnes's pulse boomed in her ears. With no time to prepare herself, such yearning filled her that she had to grip her hands together to keep from throwing herself at him. Why had she become such a dunce around him? Why couldn't she think of anything at all to say, when they had once talked so easily?

He cleared his throat. His eyes were impossibly blue. "Miss St. James. May I have a word?"

Her tongue stuck to the roof of her mouth and her lungs seemed to stop. *Merciful God. What about?*

She must have looked panicked, for he put up one hand and added, "Only a word. I shan't impose on you any more than that."

Just hearing his voice made her eyes prickle, but Agnes nodded and followed him to an alcove near the stairs.

"Thank you. I've not forgotten what you said the last time we spoke," he said formally. "I only meant to assure you that… I regard everything that happened between us as utterly private. I haven't told anyone."

She blinked. "Told anyone?"

An endearing little frown touched his brow. "No."

Did gentlemen go around telling other gentlemen after they made love to a woman? Heaven help her, perhaps they did. She hadn't thought of that. "I would hope not!"

Her horrified tone seemed to startle him. "When we met earlier, with Mrs. Ramsay, I sensed you were alarmed by my presence. I only wished to reassure you… I would never breathe a word."

She nodded, feeling stupid and miserable again. "Oh, I see. Thank you."

He exhaled and ran one hand over his head. "I'm sorry," he said in a low, rapid burst of words. "I'm sorry for that night. I never intended…"

When he closed his mouth, looking pained, Agnes swallowed the lump in her own throat. "Of course," she whispered. "I also apologize. I didn't intend any of that to happen."

His shoulders fell. "Can we be civil again?"

Involuntarily she glanced up. He'd moved closer as they lowered their voices, and his face was very near hers. His face, which she had kissed and touched and held close. He was unbearably handsome. And now he wanted to be civil, when her heart still leapt and ached every time she saw him. "Have I been uncivil?"

He recoiled, color brightening his cheeks. "I never said that."

"Then why do you wish to be civil *again*? If you had been uncivil, that would be entirely within your province to change. That question means you think I've been uncivil, yet I cannot think how I was."

His mouth hardened. "That's not what I meant."

"But that's what you said." Agnes fixed her eyes on the

silver pin in his neckcloth to avoid his brilliant blue gaze. "And it's the second time you claimed that what you said wasn't what you meant."

"Because I canna seem to express myself competently around you," he exclaimed with a spark of temper.

"Believe me, I've noticed," she said before she could stop herself.

He jerked, startled.

"What did you really mean?" She was tired of being on edge around him. "Say it plainly, if you please."

He stared at her, perplexed or frustrated or annoyed— Agnes couldn't tell which. She only knew she wanted to smooth away his frown with her thumb and hear him say something simple, something kind, something ruefully amused about how they always seemed to be off-step to each other—

"There you are," said Drew behind her, making her jump.

She spun around. "Aye, here I am. What of it?"

"I'm supposed to keep an eye on you." Her brother, no fool, narrowed his eyes, looking between the two of them. "Are you unwell?"

She flushed under his scrutiny. "I've a—a headache. Will you send for a chair so I can go home?"

Drew looked torn. "You shouldn't go alone. I'll take you…"

That would mean Winnie and Bella also would have to come. Agnes imagined their impatient and pestering curiosity, wanting to know why their evening had to be cut short as well, and shook her head. "A sedan chair will be safe enough."

"I'll see her home," said Felix Duncan.

She panicked at the thought of being alone with him in the dark for the half-hour walk home. "Oh, no!" Agnes scurried to her brother's side. "Don't make Bella and Winnie leave. And you deserve a night of dancing."

"Duncan could," he began, but she shook her head.

"Please don't ask Mr. Duncan," she whispered urgently.

Drew gave her a long, searching look, and then gave his friend an even longer one. "Aye," he said at last. "Duncan, would you be so kind as to keep an eye on my younger sisters while I take Agnes home?"

"Of course," was the stiff reply.

Agnes made herself turn. He stood straight and tall, his jaw set, his gaze fixed on her brother. "Good evening, Mr. Duncan." She bobbed a curtsy.

"Miss St. James." He bowed his head without looking at her again.

And Agnes followed her brother down the stairs, head held high but hands in fists, wishing she had spent the night at home in the broom cupboard.

Chapter Seven

F elix's desire to go to Stormont Palace had waned considerably, but there was no avoiding it now.

During a game of golf on the Leith links, St. James invited Alex Kincaid and Adam Monteith along on the trip. Felix had been debating wriggling out of it, but now realized it was to be a jolly holiday outing. St. James was already giving him long, suspicious glances whenever Agnes was mentioned, and if he begged off he would probably be directly asked.

He took the coward's way out, fearing what he might give away if confronted, and took cover in teasing his friend about Ilsa Ramsay. He won five shillings off St. James, who twitched like an eager rabbit at every mention of her name and sent two balls into the tall grass on poor swings.

But he was not as successful in deflecting his father. Displaying the uncanny knowledge of his activities that always irked Felix, Lachlan Duncan sent a note: *Dinner tonight.* And when Felix arrived—for it was a summons, not an invitation—his father said bluntly, "I hear you're going to Perth."

Glass in midair, Felix gave a brusque nod.

"Why?"

"Why not?" he returned evenly. "I've just finished the Buchanan case and relish a change of air."

"Hmph. That was some fine work, Buchanan." Lachlan refilled his glass. He never asked about Felix's cases because he always seemed to know everything about them. "Why Perth?"

"St. James needs to have a look at a house there."

His father speared a bite of fish and chewed, watching him shrewdly. "A house related to the Duke of Carlyle?"

Damn it. St. James had asked him not to mention that around town, wanting to cling to his remaining weeks of ordinary life. But now Felix realized who one of his father's spies was. "You've been gossiping with David MacGill," he said with an admonishing *tsk*. MacGill was the Carlyle solicitor in Edinburgh, and St. James had called on him.

"Gossiping! People tell me things."

"They ought not to."

Lachlan grunted. "I don't make 'em. But my own son tells me nothing, so I've no choice but to listen to others."

"On the matter of the Duke of Carlyle, you'd best only listen and not talk."

Lachlan rolled his eyes impatiently. "I know that, lad."

Felix put down his fork, turning serious. "All right. What do you want to know?"

"'Tis true, then? He's heir to the duke?"

"It is. But he doesn't want it widely known." Lachlan raised a brow. "He only discovered it two months ago. Can you imagine going from being a humble soldier to the heir to one of the greatest titles in the kingdom? He's the heir, aye, but one still in leading strings as far as the estate goes. I daresay the duke's attorney sent him on this errand to Perth to see how he manages it."

"Stormont Palace is a large estate."

"And so negligible to Carlyle that no one has visited it in

over twenty years. It may be the smallest property the duke owns."

Lachlan acknowledged that with a nod. "And why are you going?"

Felix's gaze veered back to his plate. "He's taking his family—also as a test, I suppose, for them to see a small bit of what's to come. He invited some mates to make the party more... festive."

Lachlan grunted again. Felix unconsciously braced himself, knowing this reasonableness could only last so long.

"I hear the sisters are pleasing lasses," said his father.

Felix flaked off a large bit of fish and shoved it into his mouth to avoid answering with more than a noncommittal shrug.

"I also heard you danced with one of them."

He took his time chewing. "You heard wrongly, then."

He had asked Agnes to dance, but they'd got distracted. And now she would hardly speak to him. He stabbed a sprout.

"No, no," murmured his father thoughtfully. "That's right. You didn't dance. You drank whisky with one of them."

Only by a miracle did Felix not choke on the sprout. He abandoned eating and reached for his wine. "What a dull life your spies must lead. Why would such a thing interest you at all?"

Lachlan pointed his knife at Felix. "It interests me when my only son drags himself into my offices, looking like he's been keelhauled in the firth, to say he owes a woman the protection of his name—a woman who was not Miss Hill, whom we both agreed would make a fine bride. *Mighty* interesting, that is."

Felix drained his glass at the mention of Catriona Hill. He'd danced with her again, hoping that would somehow strike some spark between them, but it had not. He motioned for the footman to pour more wine. Lachlan watched in silence, then told the servant to leave. "Well?" he prompted when the door closed.

"Well, what? I did not drink whisky with Miss Hill, nor propose to her. Guilty on both counts."

"And the next day you felt obliged to offer this unnamed whisky-drinking lady marriage." Lachlan paused suggestively, but Felix said nothing. "That lady was one of the St. James girls, wasn't she?"

Felix shrugged. "Does it matter? I've already told you the proposal was rejected."

"So why are you going to Perth with her?" exclaimed his father.

"I'm not going to Perth *with her*."

"You're going, she's going. Sounds the same thing to me."

"It's not," said Felix testily.

Lachlan slammed a fist on the table. "Why can you not be honest with me?"

"Why?" Felix knew his voice was rising. "Why must you know everything I do, before I could possibly have a chance to tell you myself? Why do you monitor my every movement? Why do you need to know this?"

"Because I buried all five of your brothers and your mother, too!"

"Am I to blame for that?" he snarled in response.

Lachlan went still, breathing hard. "Nay. But you're all I have left, lad. I care for you and for your happiness."

Felix subsided, still seething but now miserable as well. "There's nothing to tell about any lady. If there were... I would tell you."

His father turned to his plate, pushing the fish around with his fork. "You like this one, though."

"It doesn't matter," he said with a quiet sigh.

She doesn't like me.

. . .

To Agnes's relief, the trip to Stormont Palace began well.

All four gentlemen rode while the ladies went in carriages. When they stopped for the night, Felix barely said a word to her, and when they reached Stormont Palace, he completely avoided her.

She should have been pleased, and instead she had to listen to her sisters' gales of laughter after dinner as he cut up with Alexander Kincaid, whose family had been friends of theirs for years. He was in jolly high spirits tonight— everyone was. The sound of their banter and laughter carried well in this drawing room, bouncing off the high, ornate ceiling and the many tall windows and the polished parquet floor. Agnes was as far from the elegant circle of sofa and chairs as she could get, yet still heard every word Felix said.

Her mother came away from that end of the room with a smile, shaking her head. "I'd forgotten how amusing those lads could be," she said with a little laugh. "They always were such scamps."

"Well, they're grown now," muttered Agnes. "People change."

"Of course." Her mother gave her a mild look. "You seem out of sorts."

Of course she was. She'd already abandoned Ilsa after her friend started talking about how grandly she would live, and the gentlemen she would meet, as sister of a duke. Stormont Palace was proof of that—a veritable castle, where actual queens and kings had once visited, where servants responded to one's every need, where the wine at dinner alone must have cost what Mama spent at the market in a month. Agnes had never seen such a grand house, let alone been a guest in one. It was intimidating.

Her next companion, Winnie, abandoned her for Bella, Felix and Alex. Her sisters were thrilled by everything about this party—the escape from Edinburgh, the male company, the vast beautiful house and grounds begging to be explored.

Winnie was sure the house must be haunted, and was already plotting how they could search for ghosts. Bella had spotted a maze. There was no end to what her sisters might persuade them all to do.

Even Mama, so practical and economical at home, was rapidly falling under the spell of this beautiful home. Agnes couldn't remember the last time her mother had been this pleased and relaxed—it was surely before Papa's death, though. And as happy as she was to see her family so delighted...

"I'm tired," she said, and went to bed.

In her room—she had her own, while Winnie and Bella wanted to share—she rested against the door and covered her face with both hands. Perhaps she shouldn't have come. Perhaps she ought to have stayed in Edinburgh to manage the shop, instead of leaving it to Mr. Battie, their bookkeeper. She didn't belong here in this sumptuous manor. And why oh why did Drew have to invite so many gentlemen?

Agnes sighed. That was unfair. Her brother deserved a holiday in the company of his friends. She could endure Felix's presence for a week or two without breaking down in a nervous fit. It would be selfish beyond belief if she let her tormented feelings about Felix Duncan seep out and spoil the entire sojourn.

And, of course, the questioning would be intense if she let her emotions show; her family was a close one, which made them nosy. No. She took a deep breath. She might be a spinster all her days, but she would stop moping over what might-have-been; it was not-to-be and she accepted that.

For the next few days she did an admirable job of it, if she did say so herself. Felix kept his distance and she repaid him with formal politeness when they did speak. None of that bright spark lit his gaze when he looked at her, and she made sure her own face was serene whenever he was in view. She was feeling rather proud of herself...until Bella devised a race to the center of the estate's maze, with the victorious team winning a new bonnet and a bottle of local whisky.

Each team would be one lady and one gentleman.

She hoped against hope that Mr. Monteith or Alex would draw her name from her sister's upturned hat, but when the teams separated, she was left standing with Felix.

Agnes avoided his gaze for a moment. Bella was chattering to an amused Alex, while Mr. Monteith was listening with rapt attention as Winnie explained her strategy. Men tended to look like that whenever Winnie spoke. And Ilsa was positively glowing at Drew, who was openly entranced by her. Agnes had been both amused and nonplussed by that development.

Finally she faced her partner. Without a word, without expression, he showed her the slip of paper bearing her name.

"Yes, of course." She sighed. "Everyone else is paired off, I presumed I was with you."

His gaze didn't waver. "Shall we choose the site of our attack?"

The maze was shaped like a star, with each of the five points an entrance. Bella had marked start lines at all of them and left the teams to choose. Winnie and Mr. Monteith were running to the left, Bella and Alex had already taken the nearest point and Drew and Ilsa were heading around the right of them.

"This way." Agnes followed Drew and Ilsa.

"Not the left? Two parties have gone right, we'll run into them."

"I know my sisters," she argued. "We stand a better chance against Drew."

"That's true," he said thoughtfully. "No sense of direction, that one."

Without thinking Agnes smiled. "He likes to win, though, and he's got Ilsa."

His vivid eyes flashed her way. "Aye, but we make a better team."

Agnes's smile faded and she picked up the pace, striding to the open point beyond Bella and Alex. Drew and Ilsa had disappeared behind the maze. Mama was waiting on the terrace with Mr. Watkins, the estate manager, to signal the start. Felix stopped beside her and they waited in awkward silence.

"Could we forget what happened and begin anew?" he said in a sudden rush.

Heat rolled up her face. *Forget*. That night had been carved deep into her memory. "Is that even possible?"

"Yes," he exclaimed. "It is for me. I hope for you also."

In the distance Mama called, "Is everyone ready to begin?" Excited shouts from her siblings and their partners rang out.

"You were right to reject me," went on Felix. "I shouldn't have proposed—"

She swung to face him in shock.

"That day," he finished. "I was ill—felt like death that morning—"

"Then why did you?" she burst out.

He was pale. "I thought it better to act quickly, so you wouldn't believe I didn't care. But I made a terrible case and deserved to lose. I'm sorry for it."

Mr. Watkins blew the hunting horn and automatically Agnes started forward, Felix beside her. "All I ask is to apologize for that. If you can accept it, we might move on to…"

"To what?" she asked when he hesitated.

"To what might have happened if I'd handed off the flask of whisky and led you out to dance that night."

It was so like what she herself had wondered and wanted that Agnes was struck silent.

She had also spent too much time wishing they'd merely danced That Night.

The morning he came to see her, she *had* hoped he'd come for a good reason.

And he *had* looked terrible—was he truly ill, and not sick with dread?

If she hadn't been so mortified by his grim appearance, would she have been poised enough to ask *why* he was proposing?

They were still moving through the maze, turning left again and again, even though she wasn't paying attention and had no idea where they were going.

"You were ill?" she asked at last.

He nodded. "Hideously. My valet deserves extra wages, I was so wretched. The fever lasted five days."

She thought about that as they headed down yet another left turn. It felt like they were going in a circle, driven by the tall hedge that surrounded them and hid everything else from view. There was only one choice to make, even if she found it unsatisfactory.

Just like with Felix.

She stopped. He also stopped, right in front of her. He regarded her seriously, not joking, not annoyed, not drunk or ill. Just...waiting.

She *had* liked him—very much.

She *had* wished things hadn't gone so horribly wrong.

She *did* still find him unbearably attractive, and if he really had been in the grip of fever...

"When you say 'begin again,' what do you mean by that?"

His eyes brightened with cautious hope. "As it was in Agnew's. And at the start of... that evening."

She bit her lip. "What do you hope will happen this time?"

"A stroll." He put up his hands innocently. "A friendly conversation."

"Friendly?"

Some of the color came back into his face. "To begin with, aye."

"And then?" It felt rude to ask, but Agnes didn't want to risk another misunderstanding.

"If all goes well... We'll see."

She looked at him uncertainly. That sounded...risky.

He exhaled, hands on his hips. "I wish... I want..."

"What?" she whispered. "Can you not just tell me? I never know what to think."

He looked at her. "And then this," he said, and stepped forward, taking her face in his hands and brushing his lips over hers.

It was light, quick, a surprise. It was *wonderful*. It was everything she'd replayed in her mind over and over, the way he kissed her That Night before they both went mad.

He was already releasing her and starting to step back when Agnes seized the front of his jacket and pulled him back to kiss him again.

His arms went around her and he kissed her back, so stunningly sweetly she didn't want to back away. And then the kiss deepened, and her arms wound around his neck and his hands moved over her and she lost all sense of time and place as he made love to her mouth.

By all the saints, he could kiss. Agnes had thought so at the Assembly Rooms, but had convinced herself she didn't actually remember it, that her mind had been so hazed by drink she was no judge of anything.

Today, she realized she'd got it backward. She didn't remember how *good* it had been.

"Agnes," he breathed when it finally ended. "Agnes. My God." Head spinning, Agnes rested her forehead against his shoulder as he brushed more kisses over her temple. His hand was on her back, his fingers tangled in her hair. She liked the feel of this too much—his arms around her, his body against hers, his low voice in her ear.

Suddenly it was obvious why she'd been so wicked with

him. It wasn't the whisky's fault at all—it was *her*, and the way she lost all sense every time he touched her.

With a jerk she stepped back. "I accept your apology," she said breathlessly. "Any of them—all of them. We can try to make a new beginning."

"Good," he rasped, his chest heaving. His face was sharp and focused with—with—*desire*, she realized. It made her feel hot and giddy and frightened all at once.

"We're going to lose," she blurted. "The race."

His gaze didn't waver. "Does it matter?"

Her blood seemed to be fizzing inside her veins. If she took a step forward, he would sweep her back into his arms, kiss her senseless, caress and hold her until she lost her mind again. And she would let him, because she wanted him to.

Panic stirred inside her at how much she wanted him to do that. She had to save herself, *from* herself.

"It matters to me!" She turned and bolted down the path. Felix called out, but Agnes didn't stop.

Shrieks of glee and frustration sounded over the tall hedges. Left and right she went, until she was hopelessly turned around and alone and glad of it. She hated to lose, but her heart was pounding and her hands trembled and she couldn't quite believe what she'd done—let alone what she would have done if she hadn't run away. She didn't know how to control her response to him.

She had to figure it out, though, because he kissed like the man of her dreams and made her laugh and had the finest legs any man was ever born with. She felt warm just thinking about his hands, strong and elegant and so very capable and wicked… How would she ever keep her composure over the next few days, seeing him every day, staying under the same roof?

She shivered, half in exhilaration, half from nerves. This was going to be a harrowing visit.

Chapter Eight

That night Winnie almost tripped over herself to tell Agnes and Bella what she'd seen when she and Mr. Monteith reached the center of the maze. As Agnes had foreseen, Ilsa and Drew won the race, but that was not the exciting part.

"Drew was kissing Ilsa!" Winnie reported in eager whispers. "Like he meant to eat her up!"

"And she let him?" demanded Bella.

Winnie nodded. "Clung to him like a barnacle."

Bella looked at Agnes, wide-eyed. "Did you know he fancies her?"

Agnes squirmed. She'd noted her brother's attraction, and Ilsa's corresponding interest, in Edinburgh. "I suspected, a little…"

Bella smacked her arm. "And you didn't tell us?"

"What was there to tell?" Agnes defended herself. "Some flirting. It could have meant nothing."

Winnie's mouth was hanging open. "After we tried so hard to find Drew a wealthy Scottish girl! How could you not tell us he's already found one?"

"He hasn't!" Agnes frowned at her sister. "Ilsa doesn't want to go to England."

"But if she's in love—"

"And Drew thinks he must marry a proper English lady," Agnes interrupted. He'd told their mother that the Duchess of Carlyle wanted him to settle down, and meant to introduce him to suitable ladies when he returned to England. Mama worried he'd given the duchess too much control of his life, but she was helpless to stop him.

"But if *he's* in love," exclaimed Winnie forcefully, "why can't it be?"

Her sisters were such romantics. "It's not always that simple."

Bella expelled her breath in an exasperated sigh. "But sometimes it is! If Drew can't figure out how to marry the woman he loves, he'll be a sad sort of duke."

"Aye," agreed Winnie. "And as for Ilsa, why, taking on Drew can't be more scandalous than making up a pony stall inside her house."

Bella giggled. "Who but Drew would find that amusing? Really they are perfect for each other!"

Agnes jolted. "Really?"

"Of course," said Winnie. "Imagine how dull he'll become if he marries a prim English girl. With Ilsa he has a chance to be *happy*."

She was still thinking about that when they visited Perth a few days later. Everyone but Drew—who had to study the ledgers—and Mama—who wanted a quiet rest—went to see the town. Winnie and Bella were eager to visit the millinery shop, ostensibly so Ilsa could choose a new bonnet as her prize for the maze race.

After the shop, they stopping for tea and cakes, and then Ilsa suggested a walk. Alex and Mr. Monteith begged off, wanting to visit a local landmark, leaving Felix to accompany the ladies to the park.

Winnie and Bella were chattering away about Ilsa's beautiful new hat, while Ilsa listened with a smile. She always indulged their chatter, whether it was about gossip or fashions or an exciting event. Agnes was more likely to scold them for chattering when they should have been sweeping the shop floor. Ilsa would make a better sister to them than she did, she thought with a pang. Perhaps that's why they wanted Drew to marry her.

Felix was watching her. She hesitated, then bent her head in silent invitation. Since their new beginning, he had treated her with polite ease. It calmed her nerves and gave her a chance to remember how very much she liked his attention. And the few times she caught him watching her with heat in his gaze... the sparks of attraction were stronger than ever.

He walked forward to join her. It felt as though a hundred eyes must be upon them, but a stealthy glance around showed none. Behind her, her sisters were still raving over the lovely gloves Bella had bought and discussing the perfect angle of Ilsa's new hat.

"Did you not find anything to suit you in the shop?" asked Felix as they walked. "Kincaid and I expected to be staggering under a load of parcels."

Agnes smiled. Drew had given each girl some money, but as usual she saved hers while her sisters spent theirs. "No. I'm not such a fine lady as that."

"Ah." Another few paces, then he said, "Perhaps a cricket bat would be more to your taste."

She was startled into a laugh. "I never could bat! Some golf clubs, though..."

His head snapped around. "Clubs!"

"I like golf," she said even as her face grew warm.

"Aye, aye," he murmured. "I do as well."

"I remember you and Drew used to play all the time as boys."

A faint smile curved his mouth. "Still do. We played a fort-night ago."

"Of course." Because they were such good friends. She took a deep breath. "Mr. Duncan, may I ask you something?"

His face went still. They were walking briskly along, she holding her shawl around her and he with hands clasped behind his back. "Anything," he said. "Always."

Agnes glanced back. The other three had fallen behind. "Do you think my brother fancies Mrs. Ramsay?"

He stumbled, almost falling on his face. "What?"

"You heard. Do you?"

"That's not what I expected you to ask," he muttered. "I don't think it's my place to talk about that."

"Why not? He's my brother."

His face was deep scarlet. "It's not something gentlemen discuss."

At that Agnes snorted with laughter. "Please! I used to play cricket with you *gentlemen*. I know you used to talk about which girls had prettier bosoms or daintier ankles—"

"Stop," he growled.

"I can't believe any of you have changed so much since then—"

"No!" He put his hands over his ears. "I beg you!"

Still laughing, she gave his shoulder a push.

"What?" Now he was laughing, too, his face still crimson. "It's a matter of honor between gentlemen!"

"Is it? Hmm." She tapped her chin. "So unlike ladies."

"What?" He glanced sideways at her in startled interest. "Ladies discuss…?"

"Gentlemen? Of course." She smiled, remembering how she and Ilsa had discussed *him*.

"Pray tell, Miss St. James."

"Tell?" She raised her brows at him. "When you won't share even a word? Never!"

He laughed.

"All right," she said. "Don't repeat anything he told you. Do you *suspect* he likes her?"

"Confidentially, between us?"

"Of course."

He glanced back at the other three women, now admiring Bella showing off her new gloves with elaborate poses. "Aye, I do."

Agnes nodded thoughtfully. She also suspected Ilsa was falling for her brother, but Ilsa kept insisting she wasn't looking for another husband. Her first one had been strict and cold, refusing to allow her to go out or do things she enjoyed. Despite living in the same town for years, Agnes had never met Ilsa before she was widowed, and Ilsa had once confided that it was the first time she'd been allowed to go wherever she wished. What would Ilsa do, if Drew fell in love with her?

Drew, on the other hand, was almost a stranger to Agnes. In the last twelve years he'd been home only a few weeks. Agnes had no idea what her brother felt and thought.

"Does she care for him?" Felix asked.

"Mr. Duncan," she exclaimed in exaggerated indignation. "You said a gentleman would never discuss such a thing!"

"And see how easily you persuaded me to do it," he shot back, smiling.

She grinned. "Such an effect!"

"Aye," he said lightly, but his gaze was fraught. "You do have a wondrous effect on me, Miss St. James."

Pleasure bubbled inside her. She had missed this; she didn't feel ignored or uninteresting when talking with him. "That could be taken many ways."

"Please answer the question," he said. "Don't attempt to change the subject."

Agnes laughed. "Fair enough. Aye, Mr. Duncan, I believe she does."

"I thought as much."

"And now that we've concluded that line of inquiry, what

did you think I was going to ask when you agreed to answer? You did say I could ask anything, always. I wish to exercise that prerogative."

His high cheekbones were awash with color again. "Lord above, Miss St. James, do you perchance read law books under your blankets at night?"

"Women aren't allowed to read law."

"And I know why," he retorted. "Every man at the bar would be routed, if they admitted ladies." Agnes laughed. "I thought you might ask something... er... related to more personal matters."

She raised her brows and waited.

"Something pertaining to... That Night."

Now *her* face was red. "Such as?"

"I don't know," he said softly. "There's plenty I wonder about."

Her heart skipped about three beats. She had to clear her throat to speak. "I can't imagine why." His brows snapped together. "I mean—perhaps it ought not to be examined too closely, because it was not planned or intended by either of us, and there was nothing behind it except—" *Lust. Attraction. Desire.* She bit her lip. "Whisky," she finished awkwardly.

He stopped walking. "You think that's the reason?"

"Well—obviously..."

He was stared at her as if she'd said something rude and offensive.

Agnes looked down, feeling stupid again. And while she stood there, flummoxed and unsure, Bella rushed up. "What are you discussing so somberly?"

She flushed scarlet. "Nothing!"

Her sister inhaled loudly. "Is it... *you know what*?"

"*You know what?* No, I don't know," said Felix with a rueful laugh. "I don't know anything at all. Enlighten me."

"Bella!" Agnes glared in threat. "We'll talk about that later." Ilsa was *right there* and would be mortified if she overheard them discussing how attracted she might or might not be to Drew.

"All right," exclaimed Bella defensively. "It looked like a very cozy conversation, though, and I wondered if—"

"Mr. Duncan doesn't want to be drawn into your intrigues."

"Intrigues!" Bella looked between the two of them. "What *were* you talking about, to be in such a mood?"

Felix looked at her, one eyebrow quirked questioningly.

Flustered, heart hammering, her mind awhirl, Agnes blurted out, "Nothing important. I'm going to walk with Ilsa." And she turned on her heel and hurried back to her friend, leaving Felix to watch her go with a sudden frown.

Chapter Nine

F elix Duncan lay in bed, arms folded behind his head, and stared at the dark canopy above him.

All his life people had told him he was a clever lad: tutors, his father, professors, grateful clients, even judges. Tonight, he was fairly certain those people had lied to him.

But he was a good lawyer. He'd been taught to make logical arguments at his father's knee before he was out of shortcoats. *Think before you speak*, Lachlan had lectured him; *speak before you act, and when you do speak and act, do it decisively.*

Too late for that, Da, he thought darkly.

Tomorrow they would return to Edinburgh. His golden chance to repair the rift between him and Agnes was almost over. Things had been going well, until Perth—and she'd barely spoken to him since.

It was time to analyze the situation with the logical side of his brain. *Think*, he commanded himself.

It was shocking—and lowering—to learn Agnes believed he'd only made love to her because he was drunk. Whisky hadn't made him want to kiss her and hold her and lay her across his lap so he could feast on her and pleasure her.

Whisky had made him forget that he wasn't supposed to *do* it, no matter how much he wanted to, but the *desire* to do it had preceded the whisky by weeks.

But it was a marked departure from his earlier behavior. Before, he'd been a gentleman, charming and flirtatious yet strictly respectable. And she no doubt thought he would continue to behave like a gentleman when she took his arm at the Assembly Rooms. Which he would have done, probably, if she hadn't asked if he meant to kiss her.

The memory of that was enough to make him hard again. He could still hear her voice, gasping *yes* as he cupped her breast. Could still taste her skin, so warm and soft and flushed with desire. Could still feel her arms around him, her fingers digging into his shoulders, urging him on. Could still remember how hot and wet she was when she climaxed around his fingers—

With a curse he flung himself out of bed and opened the window, letting in the cold wind.

If she could see him now, she wouldn't doubt how much he wanted her, he thought wryly. But Agnes didn't want to discuss what had happened. Aside from his apology in the maze, that topic had ruined every conversation with her since.

And he should know why. Didn't he hate it when his father kept battering away at something he didn't want to speak of? His efforts to apologize were only making her uncomfortable. Felix inhaled deeply, the frigid air bracing to both mind and body. He had to let it go.

However, they *had* managed to talk about other things; she'd even laughed and punched his arm. There lay the foundation of his hopes.

A thump sounded overhead. Felix glanced upward, but nothing followed. He shrugged it off, and was getting back into bed when a door slammed.

He sat up. Stormont was an old house, with thick walls of

stone and stout oak doors. That door had slammed rather hard for him to hear it.

A moment later he heard voices—female voices, high and excited. He recognized one as Bella's, and started to relax again, until someone started pounding on a door—not his—and crying, "Agnes! Agnes, open the door! Are you awake?"

Felix was out of bed and across the room before he remembered he was naked. With a curse he yanked a discarded shirt over his head and clutched his plaid around his waist, and inched open his door.

Out in the corridor huddled Bella and Winnie, swathed in shawls over their nightdresses. They were knocking on a door two down from his. As he watched, it creaked open. "What?" Agnes whispered.

Felix was struck dumb. God, she was beautiful. Her black hair tumbled down her back almost to her waist in loose curls. Her feet were bare beneath her nightgown, and the memory of her satiny soft legs parting for him flashed across his mind like a crack of lightning.

Stop, ye loon. With a shudder he started to close his door, but it creaked and all three women whirled.

"Mr. Duncan!" The candle shook in Winnie's hand, casting flickering shadows over her pale face. "Did you hear something, too?"

He paused, looking to Agnes, who made a small, puzzled motion. "Like what?"

"A thud, or a scrape, or something frightening," whispered Bella anxiously. "From above?"

It was as cold as a grave in the corridor, and there was an eerie whistling sound. "I'm sure 'twas an owl on the roof, or a rat in the rafters."

Bella gave a little scream and Winnie jumped. "It sounded far too big to be a rat!"

Another door creaked open. "What's the trouble?" grumbled Alex Kincaid, sticking out his head.

The girls erupted in a babble. "Did you hear it, too? It seemed to go on for a long time. Tell me someone else heard what I heard!"

Alex blinked in bemusement. The door on the far side of Agnes's opened and Mrs. St. James stepped into the corridor, wearing a thick dressing gown and a cap over her hair. "What's this?" she asked sharply.

"Mama, we heard something!" cried Bella, abandoning all subtlety. "In the attics!"

Punctuating her words, a high distant shriek sounded, making the girls cry out and grab each other. Felix looked upward, perplexed. Winnie had been talking of ghosts since they arrived, especially at dinner tonight, but this was the first sign of anything supernatural.

"Have we a real ghost?" demanded Adam Monteith, appearing out of his room beyond Felix's. "I say, let's have a look!"

Winnie uttered another little scream at the word *ghost*. "No! Could it be? Is this house haunted?"

Felix looked again at Agnes. "I doubt it."

"Then what made that noise?" demanded Bella. "You heard it, too, didn't you, Mr. Duncan?"

"Aye," he said slowly. "But—"

Monteith whistled. "It's bloody cold enough to be haunted! Didn't you wish to see a specter, Miss Winifred?"

Winnie looked torn. "Well—perhaps we *should* look—"

Agnes rolled her eyes, but her lips twitched. Felix choked back a laugh. "Aye, perhaps we should." He snatched a lamp from his mantel and lit it from Winnie's candle. "Let's have a look upstairs. To set everyone's mind at ease."

On instinct he followed the chill breeze moaning softly through the corridor, to a door on a pitch-dark stair leading upward. There he paused. A block of wood held the door ajar, admitting the icy air that swirled around them.

He'd seen that here at Stormont once before, a door

propped open. He'd gone up the stairs to investigate and come out on the roof to find Andrew St. James locked in a passionate embrace with Ilsa Ramsay. Felix hesitated, not wanting to lead the whole party upon another such scene—let alone one more intimate. For one thing, St. James would probably throw him backward down the stairs.

But no light shone from above. This was a stair into the attics, not to the roof, and the temperature would curdle the blood of even the hardiest Scot. If St. James had chosen a frigid attic for his seduction and couldn't even do it quietly, he deserved to be spied upon.

He kicked aside the block of wood and led the way up. Bella and Winnie crowded behind him, along with everyone else, to Felix's surprise.

As he climbed he lifted the lamp. The light barely penetrated the gloom, but the attics appeared deserted.

"What do you see, Mr. Duncan?" whispered Winnie.

"Surely 'tis naught but a stray animal," he assured her. "I see nothing."

Monteith pushed past him, puffing out his chest. "Show yourself, foul spirits!" he called, stealing a peek at Winnie, whose face glowed with eagerness now.

No longer fearful, both girls hurried up. Felix stepped aside to let them, exchanging a brief glance with Agnes, who followed with her mother. She quirked a questioning brow, and he shrugged. Kincaid brought up the rear with another lamp, still grumbling.

The girls were chattering about ghosts. Monteith was swaggering about, peering uselessly into the darkness. The frigid breeze swirled around Felix's bare legs. If Monteith wanted to stay up here posturing for Winnie's benefit, let him.

"I see nothing." He stifled a yawned behind one hand. "No headless Highland chieftain, no lady who threw herself from the battlements in heartbreak. Not even the spirit of a badger who got trapped in the—"

Behind him sounded a long, low wail, like a dying swan. He whirled to see a towering figure lurching toward him, shimmering pale and indistinct in the weak light. With a shout of astonishment he leapt backward, nearly dropping his lamp as the girls began screaming, Monteith and Kincaid cursed, and—

And Agnes slammed against his back, her fingernails digging into his arm and ribs as she clung to him. Without thought he reached back to hold, protect, comfort her, bracing his knees and raising the lamp aggressively as the specter loomed over them. Her breath was hot on his neck, and he could feel every inch of her body plastered against his.

"Very amusing, Andrew," said Mrs. St. James dryly.

The figure went still, suddenly shrinking to mere mortal size. St. James pulled the sheet off his head. "It was meant to be terrifying, Mother."

Felix let out his breath. "Oh merciful God," breathed Agnes against his shoulder. With a start she jerked away, past her sisters scolding their brother in high-pitched voices, past Kincaid whose shoulders were shaking with laughter, past Monteith who had begun pacing with hands on his hips, past her mother who stood with arms folded and a reluctant smile on her lips.

His heart thudded hard. She'd come to him. In that moment of shock and alarm, she'd run to *him*. Incredibly, marvelously, Felix wanted to smile.

St. James was explaining that he'd meant to give Winnie a ghostly fright after all her hopeful talk of the house being haunted. To absolutely no one's surprise, Ilsa Ramsay stepped out of the deep shadows and admitted that she had helped. Ah. Felix bit back a smug grin. St. James wouldn't miss a chance to sneak off with the lovely widow, and as everyone filed back down the stairs, he did not miss the chance to rib his friend about it.

But the excitement was over. The ladies disappeared into their bedchambers and the gentlemen to theirs.

Felix closed his door and leaned against it, his pulse still racing. Christ. What an idiotic, childish prank. And yet, his mouth curved and he laughed softly. A trace of Agnes's scent lingered on his shirt, and for that alone he approved.

AGNES CIRCLED HER ROOM, too keyed up to sleep. Not that she'd been asleep when her sisters started pounding on her door, but she'd been trying.

Now she knew she'd never sleep a wink tonight. Her ridiculous brother! And Ilsa, helping and encouraging him! Maybe her sisters were right and they were a perfect match for each other.

Her smile faded a little. And perhaps she wasn't as detached from Felix as she'd been trying to persuade herself. When people started screaming and running, she'd flown to him before her head even knew where her feet were going. And he had put his arms out as if he would die to protect her.

She paced several more circuits of her room, rubbing her elbows. She'd tried keeping her distance from him, and it had only made her cross and miserable. But talking to him often left her confused; why did things always go wrong with them?

Say it plainly, if you please, echoed her own voice in her head.

She stopped at the window and gazed out blindly. Stormont Palace was beautiful, with magnificent grounds and gardens. Ilsa had pointed out astutely that Drew's future home would be like this—that *this* house would be one of his future homes. As his sister, Agnes would meet other men who lived in similarly grand houses. She could be mistress of an elegant manor like this one, with a wealthy, eligible husband.

"I don't want one of those," she murmured to herself.

So... what did she want? Or rather... *whom*?

Tomorrow they were going home. When would she have another chance like this? Too late she regretted avoiding Felix for the last several days. Before she could reconsider, she snatched up her dressing gown and put it back on. At the door, she peered out cautiously, then slipped out, her bare feet silent on the carpet. Heart hammering, she darted two doors down and rapped quietly on the oak and held her breath, waiting.

It opened with a faint creak. His eyes widened.

"May I come in and talk?" she whispered in a rush before he could speak.

Without a word he opened the door, and she slipped inside.

The lamp still burned, and she couldn't resist glancing about in interest. His room was smaller and more plainly furnished than hers. Aside from a bed and a wardrobe, there was only a small writing desk and chair.

"Can't sleep?" Felix retreated into the shadows.

"No!" She choked on a giggle. "Could you?"

"I hadn't tried yet. I suppose your sisters will be whispering about it until dawn." He shrugged into a banyan and wrapped it around himself.

Her head buzzed. She'd got him out of bed. His bed. Which was mere feet away.

Oh.

He was tying back his hair, both arms stretched behind his head, making his shoulders look very broad. "Are you cold?"

Agnes blinked, realizing she had wrapped her arms around herself. Not from cold, but from awareness. "Yes," she lied.

For a heartbeat his gaze dropped to her chest before he

turned away and pulled a blanket off the bed. His bed. The breath rasped in her ears as she hugged herself tighter, which made the linen of her nightdress pull tight across her breasts. Her nipples were tight and hard, and he'd noticed.

He swirled the blanket around her shoulders. It smelled of wool and heather and Felix. She inhaled deeply and tried not to think that the blanket was warm from his body.

"Thank you," she said. "For letting me in. It would only be fair for me to invade Drew's room and scold him for that ridiculous prank, but..."

"Of course not," Felix said in amusement. "What you really want to do is to rail against his antics and make sport of him, and I assure you I am a more appreciative audience for that."

Again Agnes laughed. Felix pulled out the chair from the desk for her and set it facing the bed. She sat, tucking the blanket around herself, and he leaned against the bed post.

"It *was* ridiculous, wasn't it?"

He lifted one shoulder. "Aye, but it succeeded. Got all of us out of bed and upstairs into the freezing attics for a fright, didn't it?"

"Are you *impressed*?" she exclaimed.

"A good prank must be appreciated," he replied, unrepentant.

"You're all mad!" she declared. "My sisters, Drew, you, even Ilsa..."

"There." He raised one finger like a lawyer in court. "There you have named the reason why your brother decided to stomp around the attics. His conspirator."

"Oh. Yes." She smiled wryly. "He likes her very much."

Felix folded his arms. "He's mad for her."

"You said gentlemen don't talk about—"

He snorted. "No need to talk! Any time an otherwise sensible man begins to act like a fool, first look to see if there's a woman. And lo, there is, one who has entranced him from the first moment he saw her."

"Why didn't you say that earlier?"

He shrugged. "Who was I to judge his feelings? Now that he's made them abundantly clear to all, though…"

Agnes laughed in spite of herself. "My sisters hope he marries her. Do you think he will?"

After a long pause, he said, "That's a complex question."

She nodded. "I understand. He's made a promise to the duchess, about marrying a suitable English lady, and plans to live there, and Ilsa has such a disgust of the English, after the trial—"

He made a noise of dissent.

"What?" She sat up a little straighter. "He's going to be a *duke*." She had only rarely said that, as if to speak it aloud made it more real. It felt like a cloud hovering above her head, ominous and threatening even if the deluge hadn't yet begun. Her brother's title would take her away from Edinburgh, the shop… and Felix.

"That generally makes women more eager to marry a man, not less."

Agnes frowned and fiddled with the blanket.

"I doubt he explicitly promised to marry an Englishwoman, and I suspect Mrs. Ramsay could change his mind about removing to England, if she chose. As for the other charge…" One corner of his mouth turned up. "*He's* not English. And it's not disgust in her face when she looks at him."

That was true. Agnes had caught Ilsa gazing at Drew with intense longing, looking a little dazed, as if she'd been bowled over by the strength of her attraction to him.

Or perhaps Agnes thought that because it mirrored her own feelings.

Felix tilted his head back and smiled ruefully at the ceiling when she said nothing. "Of course, it's entirely possible that two people care for each other, but not enough to compromise. Or perhaps their love is not equal. What one might be willing to fight through, the other might not." He glanced at her. "And then it ends in a broken heart."

She jumped. "What?"

"He may love her desperately, but if she doesn't love him enough to go with him, what sort of future can they have? Or perhaps she does love him enough to leave Edinburgh, but he cannot bring himself to defy the duchess and marry her. It would be doomed, either way."

She cleared her throat. "Aye. Love doesn't always conquer all. Sometimes it's simply impossible for two people to be together."

"Impossible," he repeated quietly.

She sucked in a shaky breath, knowing they were no longer talking about Ilsa and Drew. "Perhaps not *impossible*, but too difficult."

"Why?"

"Well—sometimes things happen that can't be forgotten…"

"And two people can never begin again."

She frowned, feeling awkward yet aroused by this intimate conversation, in his bedroom, wrapped in his blanket which was making her unbearably hot and restless.

"Is that what you're trying to tell me?" he asked when she didn't answer. "You can say so plainly."

Exactly what she had asked him to do, and exactly what she found so difficult now.

"No, I—" She was burning up. Restlessly she shoved the blanket off her shoulders. "I don't mean that. That is, I *do* mean things can't be forgotten, but one's perception of them *can* change."

He watched her in silence.

Uncomfortably Agnes rambled on. "I did mean it when I told you we could begin again. I want to. I just—I don't blame you," she added hastily. "I—I kissed you, and asked you to kiss me, and I liked it all entirely too much, which suggests that I'm—I'm—"

"Agnes." In two steps he was on one knee before her. "It suggests no such thing."

"I was drunk," she blurted out. "That's not like me!"

He raised a brow. "Because some bloody scoundrel poured you whisky."

She blushed. "Well—no," she whispered. "It wasn't just the whisky. I had wine… rather a lot of wine… and rum punch… and then the whisky."

His expression was indescribable. Agnes wanted to pull the blanket over her head. But then Felix took hold of her hand. "It still doesn't make you wicked." His thumb was making tiny circles on her palm that stirred up that treacherous wanting inside her again.

She tried to ignore it. "Why do things keep going wrong between us? Is it… unequal attraction?"

"Of course 'tis. There's no way you could find me as attractive as I find you."

He spoke so calmly that it took a moment to register. "What?" she asked stupidly. "You—what?"

He turned her hand over and stroked her knuckles. "Well, *fascinated* would be more apt a word. I can't look away, nor keep my mind off you."

Her lips parted in wonder.

Felix's gaze dropped to her hand, still in his. "I thought you'd noticed." One shoulder rose and fell, and he released her. He started to rise.

Agnes grabbed his hands in both of hers to keep him. She was afraid this moment, just the two of them being honest and open, would be fleeting. If she let it pass, she might never have another opportunity like it. "We are a star-crossed pair, each so wrong about the other."

He froze. "Are we, now?"

She nodded. "You, thinking I don't find you attractive! I, not realizing you were ill instead of angry!"

"Angry! Why would I be angry?"

"At feeling obliged to ask…" She paused, wetting her lips. "To propose."

He sank back onto his heels. "I see," he murmured. "No, I wasn't angry about that."

Her face was warm. *All* of her was warm. She wanted to fling off the blanket—and her dressing gown and nightdress. The bed was mere feet away. "I've thought terrible things about you. I'm sorry."

He brought their clasped hands to his lips and kissed the tender inside of her wrist. "I've thought terrible things of myself, too, but I accept your apology."

She tried not to shiver. His mouth on her skin was intoxicating. "But I was wrong…"

He smiled, resting the back of her hand against his cheek. "You were only wrong to think I didn't care."

A flush of pleasure flooded her. "Perhaps we both are too inclined to think something to pieces, and lose sight of the forest for the trees."

"Trees!" He pulled a face. "Individual leaves and twigs, more like."

Agnes choked on a laugh. "It *is* a relief to speak so plainly," she confided.

"I hope you always will with me. I'd rather be openly castigated than left to wallow in doubt of your feelings."

She nodded. The room seemed much warmer now, and the bed was directly in her line of sight. Speaking about those wonderful, wicked things they'd done at the Assembly Rooms was doing very bad things to her. She had only wanted to *talk* to him, but now… "Thank you," she said softly. "For asking if we could begin again. I—I was too proud, and too humiliated by my own actions. I never would have had the courage to say anything, but... I am very glad *you* did."

"Thank you for listening," he said, his voice gone low and raspy.

Agnes realized she was tilting toward him, the blanket around her waist. Felix still knelt at her feet, her hands clasped in his. He found her attractive. He hadn't proposed out of guilt. It would take almost nothing to lean forward and kiss him again... and let him lead her to the bed... and show her exactly how much he wanted her without whisky or misunderstanding to confuse things...

Mouth dry, she shot to her feet. "I did listen to you before," she said breathlessly, keeping her gaze fixed on him and not on the bed, only three steps away. "Your proposal was appalling, though."

He rolled to his feet. "Well, I *was* on death's doorstep."

She raised her brows. "And you thought that improved your chances of being accepted?"

He pretended to ponder it. "In hindsight, I suspect it did not."

She choked on another giggle, and gave a short shake of her head.

He grinned and followed her to the door. "Duly noted."

"For the next time you propose marriage," she replied teasingly, then realized what she had said and closed her mouth, mortified.

His smile faded, and his gaze was warm on her face. "Aye. I do hope the next time is more successful."

Chapter Ten

F elix returned to Edinburgh in far higher spirits than he'd left it.

On the journey home, Agnes smiled and laughed and sat beside him at breakfast. It reminded him of his father's warning, about seeing her at his table every morning.

He did like it. He liked it very much.

There was a dark moment the evening they reached the city. St. James, clearly loath to part from Mrs. Ramsay, engineered another outing to the oyster cellar, this time with Agnes. Without thinking, Felix blurted out, "Is that a good idea?" which earned him a furious look from her.

He worried that Mrs. St. James, whose goodwill he was very keen to secure, would disapprove and blame him for encouraging scandalous behavior. When he told Agnes, as they danced in the crowded, lively cellar, she beamed in relief.

"Mama will blame Drew," she told him, her lips next to his ear to be heard over the fiddle and the stomp of the dancers. "And she'll know why he did it."

Both of them glanced at her brother, who had Mrs. Ramsay in his arms. No one could miss how the air seemed to sparkle and snap between those two. Felix didn't tell Agnes that he had seen her friend leaving her brother's bedchamber in the wee hours of their last morning at Stormont Palace. Why shouldn't St. James fall in love, too? Felix saw absolutely no reason to spoil his future brother-in-law's love affair.

Instead he swung Agnes in his arms, feeling the same searing shock every time she smiled at him or clasped his hand. God above. He'd been mocking and teasing St. James for weeks about being dazzled by a woman, and look at him now.

He was still in glowing good spirits two days later when he met Hunter in Agnew's. The visit to Stormont had lasted longer than anticipated, and Hunter had had to carry the load of their clients' demands alone. Newly conscious of maintaining his income, Felix had buckled down with ruthless efficiency and concentration.

At least, he did until Hunter arrived. Uncharacteristically late, his partner crossed the coffeehouse in a few strides. "You've not heard," he said, thumping down his satchel on the opposite chair.

"Heard what?" Felix didn't look up from the document in front of him, about a case to be argued on the morrow. "About the Cameron case?"

"Another robbery." Helen came by and Hunter paused to order coffee and buns.

"Damned fools, those thieves," said Felix, still reading. There had been a flurry of break-ins during the fortnight they were away. Rewards were posted all over town. "All Edinburgh will be at their hanging."

"Aye. Any curiosity who was robbed this time?"

Felix flipped the page. "Who?"

"A silk mercer's shop in Shakespeare Square."

It took a moment to register. Felix's pencil stopped. "Whose?"

Hunter lowered his voice. "Have a guess."

It took exactly seven minutes for him to run down the High Street, across the bridge, and into Shakespeare Square. The St. James shop stood on the north end, neat and tidy, no broken windows or concerned crowd outside. Paradoxically that made him panic, and he flung open the door fully expecting to face hand-to-hand combat. "What the bloody blazes happened?" He caught sight of Agnes, her face pale and strained, and his heart almost stopped. "Are you hurt?"

With a gasping cry she bolted into his arms. And everything else faded away for a moment as his arms closed around her and he pressed his face into her hair and inhaled, holding her tight. "My *hairt*," he breathed.

"You came," she whispered at the same time, clinging to him. "You knew."

His heart soared, not just with relief but joy. His arms tightened.

And then… Then he became aware of the echoing silence in the room. Cautiously he opened his eyes and saw Agnes's mother, staring in astonishment; Agnes's brother, mouth literally hanging open; and Agnes's sister, looking smug.

He set her back on her feet and cupped her jaw. "Whenever you need me, I will come," he murmured. "Always."

She nodded, her eyes shining. He released her and cleared his throat. "What the hell happened here?"

"We were robbed," said St. James. "What just happened *here*?" He jerked his head toward Agnes.

Felix didn't care who knew he was falling for Agnes, but this was probably not the moment to make that declaration. He tried to think of something besides the feel of her flinging herself into his arms. He frowned and peered around the salon, which bore all the signs of invasion so lacking outside. Drawers had been forced open behind the counter, the wood splintered. Smashed glass from a cabinet covered the floor, and ribbons of slashed red silk lay everywhere like trails of blood. "Was anything taken?"

"If nothing was taken, I wouldn't call it a robbery, aye?" returned St. James dryly.

Mrs. St. James put an end to it by shooing them out. Felix exchanged one last intense glance with Agnes before following her brother into the street.

The crime spree had plagued Edinburgh for months now: the victims included jewelers, grocers, merchants of all stripes. Once upon a time, he'd even gossiped about it with Agnes and Ilsa Ramsay in the coffeehouse.

St. James had missed most of it, and paid little attention even once he arrived in Edinburgh, so Felix had to fill him in. St. James listened thoughtfully, then turned to examine the shop door. "This lock was opened as easily as if the villains had a key," he observed.

Felix bent down. The lock hadn't been forced. "A pick-lock?" His thoughts raced. People in Edinburgh often left the key hanging inside the door. It was convenient, to be sure— and perhaps an invitation for a thief?

But no victim had ever reported their key missing. It would have been noted when the shopkeeper locked up for the night. And if the thief could pick the door lock, why would they smash open the locked cabinets? Still, Felix filed away the thought.

"What are you going to do?" he asked.

His friend scratched his jaw. "I told Mother not to mind it too much. Seems a perfect moment for her to sell the shop and come with me to Carlyle, eh? She and the girls."

Felix tensed. "I didn't think you meant to make them go…"

"*Make* them!" The other man scoffed. "As if I could *make* them do anything! I *invited* them, to provide a better situation for my family after all these many years of being away and leaving Mother and the girls to manage on their own. But if the shop is gone, or failing, that's certainly less reason for any of them to stay."

Felix said nothing.

"Have you got anything to say about Agnes?" St. James demanded.

Not to you, he thought, and steered the conversation back to the subject of the thieves and how they could be caught.

But Felix didn't forget that the St. James family was still on the verge of leaving Edinburgh, and he was running out of time to persuade Agnes not to go with them.

AGNES WAS A SINNER FOR IT, but she was glad they had been robbed.

Not for her beloved shop, which had been cruelly violated. No money had been taken, but several rolls of gloriously beautiful silks had been stolen and several more ruined, which cost a fortune. The thieves hadn't ruined the fashion dolls she had so carefully dressed in the latest styles, but everything else had been ripped apart, smashed to pieces, or soiled.

Not for her mother's sake. Mama was by turns furious and terrified by the carnage wrought upon the shop, where she had struggled and sacrificed for so many years. Mama had given so much of herself to this shop, constantly trying to wring out a spare shilling for new shoes for one of the girls or more meat for their dinner. Years of her work lay broken and crushed on the floor.

Nor for her sisters' sake. They were briefly frightened by the intrusion, and Winnie made things worse by fretting aloud about the thieves coming back to kidnap one of them, but mostly her sisters threw themselves into the task of cleaning up and repairing the shop.

And she certainly wasn't glad for her brother's sake. Drew was determined to see the villains caught and punished, and began using his Carlyle connection to achieve that. He took off for several days on some vague business, saying he had to visit someone about a delicate matter, even though Mama asked him to stay and help her.

No, Agnes's joy was purely selfish. When Felix Duncan erupted into the shop, his face fierce, all the doubt and uncertainty that had clouded her mind abruptly cleared, and she was almost blinded by the brilliant truth staring her in the face: she was falling in love with him.

And when she'd leapt into his arms, he'd held her close and called her his heart. A warm bubbly feeling filled her every time she thought of that moment, which was often. Every time the shop door opened, jingling the bell. Every time she caught one of her sisters giving her a knowing look. Every time she stepped outside and spied Felix waiting there, reading a letter or laughing with a neighboring merchant or scratching the ears of a stray cat.

That also happened often. Once Drew left on his covert mission, it quickly became commonplace to find Felix waiting outside the shop. Sometimes she was alone, but often her mother or one of her sisters was with her, and he was always utterly charming, as if escorting the four of them at once had been his dearest hope all along.

"Mr. Duncan must have been turned off by his employer," remarked Mama one day after he had walked them to the shop before departing with a gallant bow. Winnie and Bella were still at the window, waving their handkerchiefs to him and giggling. "The man has nothing else to do."

Agnes blushed. "No, Mama, he has his own legal clients." He had told her about it on one of their rare private walks.

"Not many, if he spends his days walking from the High Street to Shakespeare Square and back."

Agnes took her time neatening the stack of sample books. "I never asked him to do that."

"Oh, I'm not suspecting you did," murmured her mother. "Now that Drew's gone, I thought you'd be glad of it."

"I am. Winifred, that window needs cleaning, now you've

pressed your face against it," said Mama. "Isabella, go upstairs and ask Mr. Beattie for today's appointments." Since the robbery, a new sign had been added to the front window: *By Appointment Only*. They had put the main salon to rights, but the upstairs, where patrons were usually received, was still in disarray.

Bella rolled her eyes and bounded up the narrow stairs behind the counter. Winnie gave Agnes a jaunty look as she fetched a cleaning cloth. "Mr. Duncan makes a handsome figure striding away," she whispered as she passed.

"Stop!" hissed Agnes, fighting back a smile. She knew he did. And an even handsomer figure coming toward her.

Her mother stopped next to her. "Mr. Duncan has improved on you a great deal, aye?"

Agnes jumped. "Mama!"

"I'm not scolding," said her unrepentant mother. "Only asking."

"Would it be terrible, if he had?" The sample books were lined up with minute precision, but Agnes kept adjusting them to avoid her mother's keen gaze.

Mama put her arm around her shoulders and bent her head to touch her forehead to Agnes's. "Nay, child. If he's the one your heart desires, no."

She sagged against her mother, half relief and half elation. "You said he was such a scamp..."

"As a lad of twelve, aye. Incorrigible!" She smiled. "But look at your own brother, playing at being a ghost. Reminded me of your father, that did, and how he would lead all those boys in games and pranks... He'd approve of Mr. Duncan, Papa would. He's grown into a stalwart fellow."

Her heart soared. "Thank you, Mama."

Mama smiled and squeezed her hand as Bella came tromping back down the stairs, list in hand. "'Tis a welcome spot of joy to see you smile like that."

Agnes laughed, and spent the rest of the day in very good charity with everyone, even her sisters and their smug looks.

She was upstairs in the offices at the end of the day, reviewing the orders to be placed with Mr. Beattie, when the bell jangled below. When she came down the stairs, her mother and sisters already wore their hats and cloaks. Felix Duncan stood listening to Mama, hands clasped behind his back, head bent attentively to what she was saying. Agnes paused on the stairs.

Her mother's words had played in the back of her mind all day. Papa *had* been fond of Felix; he'd called him a clever, bonnie lad. Drew thought him a capital fellow, for all that he and Felix mocked each other mercilessly. Her sisters thought him handsome and charming, and Mama was smiling warmly at him now. He looked at home here in her shop. Like family.

And she loved him.

As if he'd heard that thought, he turned and looked up at her. His expression remained pleasant and polite, but something sparked in his eyes that made her blush and want to run her hand over her hair to smooth it.

"Agnes, Bella has a headache. Would you finish closing? Mr. Duncan has kindly offered to escort you home," said Mama.

Bella caught on quickly. She clapped a hand to her forehead and moaned dramatically. "Oh, I do! A terrible, dreadful, painful headache!"

"We'd better go at once, Mama." Winnie hurried to open the door. "For Bella's sake."

"How I'll make it home, I'm sure I don't know," whimpered Bella. Her hand was almost covering her eyes. She wandered toward Winnie, groping blindly with one hand.

"We're going," agreed Mama. "Thank you, Agnes."

Agnes bit her lips as they bustled out, closing the door

with exaggerated care. "My goodness," she said when she was able to speak. "I hope Bella doesn't require a doctor."

"She did appear to sicken very suddenly," said Felix, his lips twitching.

"I expect she'll recover just as suddenly." She came down the rest of the stairs. "Thank you for seeing me home."

"Always." He made one of his courtly bows. "What needs doing to close up?"

She looked around. "Very little. Put down the shade in the window, and put out the lamps." Felix nodded and went to do that. Agnes went into the back and checked that the door there was locked and barred. She came back into a dim salon. Felix had extinguished all but one lamp, and with the shade down, the salon felt very intimate.

She inhaled a shuddering breath. "They know it won't take long."

He leaned against the counter. "Aye."

"So…" Her heart was racing madly. "If you're going to kiss me, you'd better do it now."

His brows went up. "And here I thought you might kiss me."

She couldn't keep from laughing a little. "Is that how you want it?"

"I'd never say no," he said.

Agnes cast a nervous glance at the door, as if her family might burst back in even though they'd schemed to leave without her. "I'm not very good at kissing gentlemen." He was the only one she'd ever kissed, and both previous times she'd kissed him, things had gone awry.

His breath hitched. "'Tis a skill like any other. Step boldly to the crease…"

She choked on a laugh and sidled closer.

"Check your stance," he murmured.

She laid her hands on his chest, feeling his hands settle lightly on her waist. Felix lowered his head.

"Now, swing from the soles of your feet," he whispered, and she went up on her toes and kissed him.

"How was that?" she asked breathlessly.

His hand slid around the back of her neck, twirling a loose curl before cupping her head. His other hand moved to the small of her back. "A good first effort. Some practice wouldn't go amiss, though, have another go…" And his mouth took hers again as his arms tightened and she melted into him, opening her mouth and letting him taste her, have her, make love to her. His hands were on her back, making her want to wrap herself around him. Shivers of hot and cold ran through her as his mouth glided down her throat, echoes of that wickedly wonderful night on the supper room sofa.

He was the one who broke away, stopping her when she would have pulled him back. His hands trembled as he cupped her jaw. "You'll drive me mad, you will," he whispered.

No, she thought in a daze, *it's the other way around.* Every kiss, no matter how small or brief she intended it to be, burst from a spark into a roaring blaze in the blink of an eye. She didn't think she would ever get tired of kissing Felix Duncan. And holding him. And laughing with him. Even just talking to him, as they had in the park in Perth and in his room, late at night.

She wasn't falling in love with him—she had already fallen, deep and hard.

"Where's your hat?" he asked as she just stood gazing at him in silent yearning. "A cloak?"

She blinked. She was in love with him. Should she tell him?

Felix swallowed hard and let go of her. "If you keep looking at me like that, your brother will tear off my head just for what I'm thinking."

His mouth on her breast. His hands under her skirt. His body, tall and lean, moving against hers. A flush raced across her skin in anticipation. "He wouldn't dare..." she whispered.

Felix took a step back. "You wouldna say that if you knew what's in my head. I'm no' makin' a muck o' this again," he warned, his voice thick. "I'm taking you home afore I lose what's left o' my wits. I'm a gentleman, lass, not a saint."

Agnes sucked in a breath, wondering what *was* in his head. Goodness, was it as wicked as the thoughts in her own mind? "Aye. Of course." She found her hat and jacket, and put them on with clumsy hands.

Out in the street, she waited while Felix locked and tried the door. The night air cooled her blood and her imagination, and she smiled ruefully as he offered his arm. *He* was a gentleman. *She* was the wanton barely in control of herself.

"I enjoyed that more than cricket batting swings," she confided as they walked.

"And ye did far better at it, too," he said with a simmering look.

She gasped in mock surprise. "I'm still faster than you in the field, I wager!"

"Aye," he said agreed, laughing. "No doubt you could catch me still."

I hope I do, she thought, and walked the rest of the way home in ebullient spirits.

Chapter Eleven

Nothing could dim Felix's good humor.

Not the weather, gray and cloudy though it was for several days. Not the crush of demands from clients. Not the thieves plaguing Edinburgh, although he did keep a keen ear out for anything that hinted at resolution.

He even went to see his father without being summoned. Lachlan barely glanced up as Felix dropped into a chair opposite his desk. "What's the trouble now?"

"No trouble at all," said Felix.

His father's brows went up. "A rare and wondrous thing."

He grinned. "Ain't it?"

That got Lachlan's attention. He straightened in his chair and pushed back his law book. "Why?"

Felix laughed. "All my life, you've scolded me for trouble. Now you fret over no trouble?"

"You only come to me when there's trouble," Lachlan replied. "Either you're lying, or you don't even know what trouble you're in."

Felix reflected. "In other words, whatever I say shall be treated as unreliable." He shrugged. "I might as well be on my way. Apologies for disturbing you." He started to rise.

"Wait," growled his father. He drummed his fingers on his desk in frustration. "Why did you come?"

Felix sank back in the chair. "You allege that I never tell you anything, and you must rely on the intelligence of others to discover my actions. So today, I've come to tell you something."

Now his father looked wary. "And it's not trouble?"

"Completely the opposite."

Lachlan leaned back and folded his arms.

"I've met a lady." Felix paused, then shook his head. "No —strike that. I've fallen in love with a lady."

His father studied the papers on his desk. "It is not Miss Catriona Hill, is it."

"No," said Felix apologetically. "It was never going to be Miss Hill."

Lachlan grunted.

"But I think you will like her very much. She's beautiful, of course, but also sensible and clever—she would make a fine attorney—and warm-hearted and very good-humored…" Felix stopped himself and cleared his throat. "I believe she cares for me as well. I want to marry her."

"Who is the fortunate lady?"

"Miss Agnes St. James." Felix waited for his father to declare that he had known all along. Not only had he divined it a few weeks ago, but Felix had been escorting Agnes to and from the St. James shop for over a week now in full view of all Edinburgh. His father was sure to have heard about that from half a dozen people.

But Lachlan merely nodded.

"All right." Felix opened his arms. "You're not surprised. What, pray, is the opinion among your friends as to her answer?"

"I've no notion," replied his father. "I've not discussed you or your love affairs with anyone. What is *your* opinion? Is she likely to accept?"

"What?" Felix stared. "I—surely you knew. You pressed me about her before I went to Perth."

"And you denied every word. Said she refused you."

He cleared his throat. "At the time, she did."

"Then I must congratulate you on arguing a persuasive appeal. A man's own self is the most difficult client to advocate for."

"One moment." Felix was stuck on his father's earlier words. "Surely you've already analyzed the match with Lord Lindow and Sir Patrick," he said, naming two of his father's colleagues and friends.

"I have not," said Lachlan, unperturbed. "After you upbraided me for it, I stopped attending to gossip about you."

He barely managed to keep his jaw from sagging open. "Entirely?"

Lachlan grimaced. "As little as possible. I hoped you would tell me yourself, if there was anything important to know. And now—" His face worked, the granite facade cracking for a moment. "'Tis very happy I am for you, lad," he finished quietly.

"You—you truly didn't know?"

Lachlan sat forward, elbows on the desk, and sighed. "You were right, aye? I've confessed it. You're my son, my only family, but you're a man and not in need of my protection."

"Protection!" Felix jolted.

His father nodded. "How else to keep my promise to your mother? You've got her mischievous spirit, and I swore to her I would keep you from harm. Without her to advise me, I feared I wouldn't be able to discern when you needed my help. But you've not needed me for years, I think." He paused. "I wish you great joy with your lady."

Felix was still stunned. "Thank you," he said after a moment.

Lachlan gave him a level stare. "So, will she accept this time?"

"I hope so." He gave a firm nod. "I believe so."

"Very good. When will I meet the lass?" His father smiled ruefully. "It's been twenty-five years since there was a woman in our family."

"Soon," said Felix, thinking rapidly. "Well—once she says yes. No point otherwise."

His father gave a bark of laughter. "No, indeed!" He sobered, then put out his hand. "Thank you for telling me. It makes my heart glad."

"Aye." Slowly Felix smiled back and clasped his father's hand. "Have I your blessing?"

Lachlan raised his brows. "You've never lacked it, Felix." There was a tap at the door, and Mathison the clerk peeked in. "Go to it, lad, and win your lady's heart."

FELIX'S good feeling persisted for several days.

St. James had gone back to Fort George near Inverness to resign his army commission, and asked Felix to see to his family in his absence. From his expression, it was obvious his friend knew he would be there anyway.

He was. He was invited to tea, and to sit with them in church. Louisa St. James's approval was evident in the way he and Agnes were always allowed to close up the shop and linger. He had learned to leave a few minutes for her to put her hair and dress back to rights before they walked home together, arm in arm.

Felix had got so far as planning where and how he would propose, when the first ominous ripples of scandal broke. He strode into Agnew's one morning, late as usual— he and Agnes had walked slowly that morning—and found a larger crowd than usual around the table where he and Hunter sat.

"What's about?" He had to squeeze through to find his partner.

"Rumors." Hunter nodded toward the man speaking. "About the thieves. Word is someone might be reaching for the pardon."

After the St. James shop was robbed, Drew had flexed his new influence and urged the Procurator-Fiscal to offer a King's Pardon to any thief who came forward and gave evidence about the crimes. Such a pardon would save a man from prosecution not only for the robberies but for every other crime he had committed in his life. The offer, printed in the papers, had caused a renewed flurry of gossip.

This seemed different, though. "But who is it?" one fellow was asking, in hushed tones.

Michael Oliphant, the bearer of these tidings, shrugged. He defended criminal charges and was frequently in and around the Tolbooth jail. "No name was mentioned."

"What clues were given?" asked Felix, to a rumble of chuckles.

Oliphant winked. "That it was a name we would all ken— a man of some prominence." Startled mutters swept the small crowd.

"The thief?" whispered Felix to Hunter, incredulous.

His partner nodded. "'Tis said there's more than one thief, and that the mastermind is a substantial man of town. Oliphant's been boasting that he's heard things from a deputy sheriff."

Felix twisted his mouth. Criminal lawyers always claimed that.

"If a prominent man is involved, we ought to be able to deduce who he is," said one man.

"The ablest minds in Edinburgh, right here," added another, eliciting more chuckles.

A few names were bandied about, analyzed for likelihood, and mostly dismissed. The more prominent the man, the more stupid he would be to risk everything by robbing shops up and down the High Street. Felix listened skeptically, until one name caught his ear.

"Deacon Fletcher."

William Fletcher was Deacon of the Wrights, a town councillor, and owner of one of the largest cabinetry shops in town. He was also the father of Ilsa Ramsay, who was soon likely to be—if Felix read the signs correctly—Mrs. Andrew St. James, the future Duchess of Carlyle.

"Fletcher," scoffed one. "He could buy and sell half this town, and send the other half to jail!" The man who'd proposed it shrugged, and the discussion flowed on.

Except in Felix's mind, where little scraps of info were tumbling together into a worrisome bundle. Fletcher made fine furniture, like the walnut bookcases and cabinets in Lachlan Duncan's law chambers, and the heavy, carved door to the offices with the good lock in it.

Felix remembered that lock. Several years ago, one of his father's clerks had been caught reading files and selling the info he gleaned from them. Lachlan had had every lock in the office replaced, even on the cabinets, and Fletcher's men had done them all. Because Fletcher was also a locksmith.

The door of the St. James silk shop had been opened as easily as if the thieves had a key. Like many in Edinburgh, Mrs. St. James left the key hanging just inside the door, in plain sight. She'd never missed it, but if someone took an impression of it… someone able to make a false key…

He retreated to a private table to dash off a quick note. Then he muttered an excuse to Hunter and went out to hire an express messenger to Fort George.

Chapter Twelve

The robbery clarified more than Agnes's feelings for Felix.

It also reminded her of how much she loved her shop. Seeing it torn to pieces was like a bucket of cold water to the face. Papa would have been furious, and devastated. Agnes was ashamed that she had lost sight of that, between the trip to Stormont Palace and her emotional tumult. And when Drew suggested they simply sell the shop, so they could go with him to England, something inside her seemed to fracture.

Drew was not going to sell her shop. She would repair it and restore it, better than ever, and when Mama gave in and left Edinburgh with Drew and her sisters, Agnes was going to take it over—as Papa would have wanted. She threw herself into it, nudging Mama to make changes, even spending her savings on new displays for the window and new glass in the cabinet doors.

It took her some time to realize that between that effort and Felix's attentions, she'd been neglecting Ilsa. Mama had agreed that she could stay with Ilsa for a month; when that ended, Agnes went home without arguing to stay longer. Ilsa would probably be glad, she'd told herself, to have more privacy to conduct her own romance with Drew, which no one bothered to deny anymore. Mama had invited Ilsa to dine with them and received her like an honored guest.

But Agnes hadn't considered that her brother had been out of town a great deal, first on his secret mission and then back to his regiment near Inverness. Agnes and her sisters still walked with Ilsa from time to time, but they saw her far less often. And even when she did talk with her friend, she couldn't bring herself to tell Ilsa about Felix.

She didn't know why; embarrassment at how it had gone wrong at the Assembly Rooms, perhaps, and a vague fear that her current happiness wouldn't last. At times it still felt like a dream that might abruptly end if she told anyone she was in love. She had never had a suitor before and had no idea how to act. Felix hadn't proposed again, or even told her he loved her. How stupid she would feel, if she told people and then his interest faded.

A customer jolted her out of that.

Betsy Steuart was one of their best customers, wife of a prosperous jeweler, and was one of the first to return to the shop to select her silks over tea and cakes. Mama usually received her, but Agnes persuaded Mama she could do it. She was ready for Mrs. Steuart with fresh tea and several carefully chosen bolts of silk.

"Have you heard the latest rumors, Miss St. James? Surely you *must*."

Agnes smiled politely. Every client probed for information about the thieves, certain that the victims knew more than anyone. "Not a bit, Mrs. Steuart."

"But Captain St. James—"

"He's not told us anything, and now he's away from town." Agnes spread out a beautiful primrose silk, printed with scarlet poppies. "This has just arrived, and would suit your coloring perfectly—"

"I hear there will be an arrest soon, and it will set the entire town on its ear."

Agnes was sick of the thieves. "I hope so. Now, if you prefer a green, we have this celadon china silk—"

Mrs. Steuart was all but falling off the edge of her seat. "They say it will be Deacon Fletcher!"

Agnes froze. "What?"

Mrs. Steuart's round, pretty face was eager with expectation. "They say he's involved with these robberies," she whispered loudly.

Her heart almost stopped. Ilsa's father! "Impossible…"

Mrs. Steuart blinked. "Is it? Why, it would be remarkable, and very shocking. A deacon and town councilor! Who could be less likely to smash in doors and rob honest people? But that is what they're saying…"

Agnes swallowed. It *couldn't* be true. "We mustn't accuse anyone without evidence. Now, about this print…" She forcibly steered Mrs. Steuart back to the silks unfurled across the table.

When the woman finally left, she ran downstairs. "Mama, I must leave," she gasped. "Immediately."

Her mother took one look at her face and nodded.

Almost running back toward the High Street, she met Felix on the bridge. "What's wrong?" he demanded.

"Ilsa," Agnes gulped. "I have to see Ilsa."

He didn't ask why, just turned around and kept pace with her. "Have you heard?" she asked as they went. "About her father?"

"Aye," he said after a pause. "I hope it's not true."

"You knew!" She stopped in her tracks. "And didn't tell me?"

He stepped closer and took her hand. "I only heard it a few days ago, as a vague guess, no accusation at all. And I sent a man straight up to Fort George with the news, just in case," he added as she opened her mouth.

All right. He had taken it seriously. "What did you tell Drew?"

"I knew nothing to tell. I only warned him there were rumors."

They had reached Ilsa's house. Felix stopped at the step. "Give Mrs. Ramsay my regards."

Agnes smiled, her heart brimming with warmth. "Thank you. I will."

"Shall I wait?"

She shook her head and rapped at the familiar door.

But there was no need for him to wait. Mr. MacLeod, Ilsa's butler, said she was not at home. Agnes bit her lip but nodded.

Something flickered over Felix's face when she came back down. "Won't she see you?"

"She's out."

His gaze jumped to the sitting room windows above them.

"She's likely sitting in a coffeehouse with Sorcha White or walking on the hill with Robert," said Agnes, feeling guilty and a bit jealous, which made her feel guiltier. *She* used to be the friend Ilsa walked with and sat in coffeehouses with. "I'll call again tomorrow."

"Aye," said Felix. "Do."

But when tomorrow came, things were even worse.

A knock sounded on the door as they were finishing breakfast. Agnes ran down to answer and found Felix. "I cannot stay," he said when she invited him inside. "I wanted to tell you Deacon Fletcher left town at dawn. The sheriff's men are at Mrs. Ramsay's house."

"What?"

Felix held up one hand. "To see if she knows where her father went, nothing else."

"I have to go!"

He caught her as she started to run upstairs. "It's only questioning. They won't arrest her."

Agnes gripped his fingers. "But we have to help."

He wrapped his other hand around hers. "She will need her friends. Otherwise, there's naught we can do."

She blinked rapidly. "Naught!"

"They'll only ask questions," he said in the same calm, forceful voice. "She'll tell them she knows nothing. They haven't even arrested Fletcher."

"But what if she *does* know something?" Agnes burst out.

Felix tensed. "Do you believe so?"

"No, but she's devoted to her father. She won't tell the sheriff anything if they intend to arrest *him*."

He turned and stared into the distance, his jaw tight. Agnes shook his arm. "What can we do?"

"Be her loyal friend," he said after a pause. "If she needs help, she'll want a lawyer."

Agne recoiled. "You think they *will* arrest her."

He put up one hand. "I don't see why they would, unless they've got evidence she was involved."

"She wasn't! But the gossips will think so. Oh, Felix, she suffered so much from the evil gossip last year. There must be something..."

"Advise her to do nothing to arouse the sheriff's suspicions. If he believes she knows nothing, he'll leave her be."

"She should sit quietly at home and insist she knows nothing of her father's criminal activities?" Agnes demanded. "She shouldn't protest his innocence, only hers?"

He gave her a look of apology. "If she wants to stay clear of trouble, yes."

Agnes knew her friend. Ilsa adored her father; she would never sit by quietly and watch him be condemned. And Agnes understood that. If someone had accused *her* papa of such a terrible thing, she wouldn't sit quietly at home, either. "Drew would do something."

Felix's brows drew together. "Then he'll do it when he returns."

"That may be too late!"

He took a deep breath and cupped her cheek. "If I know him, he'll find the fastest horse in Fort George and race back to Edinburgh. He'll be here soon."

Agnes turned her face away and said nothing.

Felix raised her hand and kissed her white knuckles. "Trust me, love. I'll come back if I learn more."

He left, and Agnes slammed the door. *Wait. There's nothing you can do. Tell your friend to say nothing as her family is torn to shreds by cruel and vicious gossip.*

Felix didn't understand. His family had never suffered a sudden fall from grace, as hers had. He had never had to endure the pitying looks, the way friends suddenly vanished, the shame of being unwelcome where you had once been at home.

There had been nothing to say or do against that when it had been her family, reeling from Papa's death and struggling to adapt to their new poverty. Perhaps she couldn't do much for Ilsa, but she *could* let her friend know she was not alone— and never would be. Agnes ran back up the stairs to fetch her hat, determined not to be turned away this time.

Chapter Thirteen

✦✦✦

F elix hadn't wanted to worry Agnes, but he was uneasy for Mrs. Ramsay.

He feverishly dug about for more information. It was the first thing St. James would want when he roared back into town, and Felix was determined to have something to tell him. He began haunting Agnew's, waiting for Oliphant or any other criminal lawyers to turn up and share what they'd heard. He even chatted up two sheriff's officers he knew, to no avail. All anyone knew was that Fletcher had disappeared, and while the man's sister and daughter claimed no knowledge of his actions or location, rumors were flying around town that they knew more than they were admitting.

When Agnes asked him, he jumped at the chance to call on Mrs. Ramsay and see for himself how she was faring—which was, not well. The sparkling, beguiling woman he'd known at Stormont Palace was gone, replaced by a quiet woman with guarded eyes.

"I thank you, sir," she murmured in response when he asked what he could do to help. "But I don't know what there is to be done."

Agnes was all but vibrating beside him. Felix tried again.

"I heard the sheriff has been here more than once. Perhaps, out of an abundance of caution, it would be wise to retain counsel."

Thanks to a loose-lipped sheriff's deputy, Felix knew they had searched her house. He'd expected that, but it was still a bad sign. And yet Mrs. Ramsay only shook her head and repeated that she had no need of an attorney.

Agnes was distraught when they left. "She's miserable," she exclaimed. "What can we do?"

"Remain a steadfast friend," he said for the tenth or twentieth time.

"Stop saying that!"

"What do you want to hear?" he demanded.

She stopped walking, flushed and angry. "Something else! Anything else. There must be *something*—"

"If there were, I would tell you," he cut in. "She's not been arrested. She's being watched, but we can't stop that. Control the gossips? Only God could, and I give even Him only half a chance in this town. You can't force aid upon her."

Tears glittered in her eyes.

Felix gentled his tone. "There's no indication the sheriff thinks she was involved in the robberies, only that she might know where her father has gone. She says she doesn't and they can't prove otherwise. I know it's hard to bear, but she's safe in her home. What she needs are friends, to keep her spirits from flagging."

A muscle in her jaw trembled. "I am her friend," she said at last, in a quiet, controlled voice, "but holding her hand and drinking tea with her isn't enough. She had to sit in silence during that dreadful trial last year, when everyone whispered that she'd had an affair with that—that horrid Englishman, and that's why he killed her husband. People called her a Jezebel and a whore, did you know?"

"I heard," he admitted, rubbing his neck. "But that was only gossip—"

"Gossip wounds!"

"She's *got* to ignore it!" he exclaimed. "She must. Anything she does will only appear to confirm it and make everything worse."

Agnes flinched as if he'd struck her. "You would make her a helpless rabbit, paralyzed in the middle of an open field for fear of attracting the notice of a hawk who is already circling overhead."

"She's not a rabbit," he said tightly. "But it is difficult, even impossible to prove a denial. Sometimes the best you can do is *not* lend credence to the accusation."

"And in the meantime, she must simply suffer all manner of slurs upon her entire family." She shook her head. "It's too much to ask a person to bear. I wish you could understand that." She turned and headed toward her house.

He caught her arm. "If there were more I could do, I would. I swear it, Agnes!"

She looked at him with unreadable eyes. "I understand. You cannot do anything. I need to think of how *I* can help my friend, because someone must." She pulled loose. "Goodbye, sir."

Felix stood on the step for several minutes after she went inside, alternating between impatience at Andrew St. James and anger at the sheriff's men. They *were* hounding Mrs. Ramsay, because they had no other leads on finding Deacon Fletcher, and only St. James, with his Carlyle connections, might be able to stop them.

He let out his breath. It had been several days since he sent the messenger to Fort George. St. James would surely be back any moment now, ready to take the action Agnes yearned to see.

Felix didn't know what that would be. But if it were Agnes in trouble, he knew he would risk life and limb to get to her side, and do everything and anything in his power to protect and comfort her.

Anything in his power.

He closed his eyes. There was one source he hadn't tried—one source he never tried. He had made a vow not to, to avoid the slightest hint of impropriety. He had always been determined to be his own man and make his own way.

But this time, it wasn't his interest at stake. He turned and headed toward Parliament Square. A clerk waved him in, and Felix closed the door.

"Has she accepted? Is the wedding date set?" Lachlan—a Lord of Justiciary who heard criminal cases from the bench and signed warrants for arrest—glanced up, a half-smile on his face.

Once raised to the bench, he had refused to discuss one word about any case that might come before him until the case was concluded. *Lives and liberty are at stake,* he would say. *No man should gain advantage over another because of his connections.*

"Not yet," said Felix. "I need to know what evidence Sheriff Cockburn has against Mrs. Ilsa Ramsay in the matter of William Fletcher."

AGNES RACKED her brain for ideas.

Felix wasn't wrong, but she couldn't do *nothing*. Holding Ilsa's hand and murmuring empty phrases about hope and solace wasn't her way; nor was it her friend's. Felix said she was safe at home, but Agnes knew that the longer this dragged on, the tighter the vise holding Ilsa would become: always suspected, unable to clear her name, hearing her father reviled from one end of town to the other but unable to defend him for fear of bringing more suspicion upon herself.

There might be little she could do, but that little she *would* do. She went to see Sorcha White and encouraged the other girl to defend Ilsa in every drawing room she visited. In the shop, she gossiped freely about the thieves and robberies, asserting to all that Ilsa knew absolutely nothing about anything, especially her father's actions, whatever those might be. She told her sisters to do the same with their friends. They might not be able to turn the tide of rumor, but they could muddy it up.

But she realized that eventually one of two things would happen. Either Deacon Fletcher would come home to face the charges, or Ilsa would break under the strain and go looking for him. Given the clandestine way Fletcher had left, Agnes thought it was more likely to be the latter.

Ilsa's butler didn't want to let her in. Agnes asked, she pleaded, she hectored. Finally the man hesitated long enough to allow her to slip past him and run up the stairs, where she found Ilsa in the drawing room.

The sight made her stop in shock. Pale, thin, nothing like her merry self, Ilsa was simply sitting alone in the room, the drapes pulled shut. "Agnes," she murmured. "How are you?"

"What are you planning?" she demanded.

Ilsa didn't flinch. "What do you mean?"

"I saw it in the papers, that your father contacted you. Was it really a confession?"

"Of course not. He's innocent."

Agnes nodded. "I know. But I also know you, Ilsa. What are you going to do?"

Ilsa looked up, a tiny spark in her eyes.

It took some persuading, but in the end she tacitly admitted that Agnes had guessed correctly. She was going to go after her father, because no one and nothing else had come to her aid.

Agnes indulged in a moment of fury at her absent brother. Where *was* Drew? He'd been gone for weeks. "Let me go with you," she begged.

"Absolutely not."

Agnes despised this helpless inactivity. "When are you leaving?"

Ilsa said nothing. A shaft of sunlight pierced a gap in the draperies and illuminated her face, stark white and bereft. Her anguish was almost palpable in the still room. Agnes thought again of her beloved father, of the blow she'd suffered when he died so suddenly and left them in such bad circumstances. People had whispered about Papa's failings as their family plummeted into poverty. It must be similar for Ilsa, but with the added torment of facing it all alone.

Agnes flung her arms around her friend. "Promise you'll be careful."

Ilsa nodded. "Would you look in on Robert? It would be a great comfort to me."

She had promised to do anything to help her friend, and here it was: walk the pony. Tearfully she nodded. "Of course! We shall walk him out every day and spoil him with apples and carrots."

When she left, she walked aimlessly. Mama and her sisters would be at the shop. Agnes knew she should go there, too, but instead she found herself in front of the Exchange.

Agnew's coffeehouse was busier than ever. She caught sight of Felix in a small group of men standing around a table, cups in hand. They were arguing; Felix slashed the air with his hand, making some point with force. One man was shaking his head, while another, familiar-looking fellow periodically nodded in agreement.

She stood staring at him. All this time, he'd been right. *Be a steadfast friend*, he'd said. That had been the most important thing all along. She'd spent days worrying about what she could do, trying to convert the women who came to the shop, when she ought to have been with Ilsa to buoy her spirits. She ought to have asked Ilsa how she could help, instead of thinking she might somehow divert a criminal investigation or shout down the gossips. And if she had listened to Felix, she would have done all that.

Felix must have felt her gaze upon him. Mid-argument, he

glanced her way. Agnes's throat tightened. She hadn't seen him since their rather frosty parting a few days ago. Never taking his eyes off her, he strode through the crowded coffeehouse to her.

"Has something happened?" he asked.

Her lip trembled, and then she reached for him. With a quiet oath he pulled her into his arms, holding her tight. Heedless of the scandalous public display they were making, Agnes clung to him, hiding her face against his shoulder.

"There, love," he whispered.

"You were right," she managed to say. "You were right and I was wrong. Oh Felix, what are we going to do?"

Chapter Fourteen

❧❧❧

F elix paced his sitting room for hours.

He had broken his pact with his father. He didn't regret it, but it had not helped him know what to tell Agnes. Too late he realized he'd been too certain there was nothing to her fears for Mrs. Ramsay. He'd expected his father to confirm it and reassure him that he'd given Agnes the right advice.

Instead, Lachlan Duncan had told him that Sheriff Cockburn, frustrated in all his attempts to locate William Fletcher, *was* contemplating arresting Ilsa Ramsay to lure her father out of hiding. Cockburn suspected she had warned her father to flee, and Fletcher had sent his daughter a letter after his flight. It looked like a simple farewell note, but some in the sheriff's office thought it was a coded message about his destination. The possibility was enough, just barely, to justify putting her in the Tolbooth for a few days.

The sheriff was already watching her house. If she tried to leave town, as Agnes believed she was planning, they would probably take her into custody.

God above, where the bloody blazes was Andrew St. James? Did Felix have to ride up to Fort George personally to fetch the man? If he wasn't back by morning, Felix would have to take up vigil outside Mrs. Ramsay's house himself.

But finally, a few minutes after midnight, the door flew open with a vehemence that almost extinguished the lamps. Grimy with dirt, gray-faced with exhaustion, Andrew St. James strode in.

IT WAS BARELY light out the next morning when a ferocious pounding woke him. Felix staggered to open the door and was nearly bowled over by the St. James girls. "Where is he?" cried Winifred and Isabella. Felix waved one hand. Agnes paused to lay her hand on his arm as her sisters rushed past.

"Thank you," she said softly. He'd sent her a note late last night letting her know her brother had returned.

Still half-asleep, Felix nodded. He and St. James had been out disturbing officials and arguing with them until five in the morning—furiously enough to please even Agnes, he thought. "Leave him to it now." He jerked his head toward St. James's room.

"What can he do that you could not?"

He scrubbed his hands over his face. Lachlan's intelligence about the sheriff's intentions had indeed spurred St. James to immediate and extreme action. Agnes might not like her brother's new expectations, but that ducal connection had been what got the sheriff and the procurator-fiscal's deputy out of bed to speak to them in the wee hours of the night, and made them listen to St. James's arguments in Ilsa Ramsay's favor. Felix thought they'd persuaded everyone to leave the woman in peace, for now. "Win her confidence, for one thing. She'll welcome his help when she rejected mine."

"But what will he *do*?"

Before Felix could answer, the man himself staggered into the sitting room, two sisters at his heels. Unshaven, eyes bloodshot, plaid wrapped around himself like a winding sheet, St. James gave Felix an exhausted look and dropped into a chair.

"Drew, what are we to do?" asked Agnes at once. "We have to help Ilsa."

"Aye," he said groggily. "Give me a moment." He reached for a discarded boot and missed. His sister kicked it toward him.

"What did you learn last night?" demanded Bella.

"Will they leave Ilsa alone?"

"What are you going to do?"

Wincing, St. James put his head in his hands. "Calm, mademoiselles," said Felix. "Let us sit down—"

"Bother that!" cried Bella. "We've been expecting you for days and days, Drew, what took so long?"

"You've got to put a stop to this," Winnie told him. "Immediately. Poor Ilsa!"

"You have no idea what she's been through."

St. James looked like he might collapse. Felix guessed he hadn't slept in days—he certainly hadn't slept last night. "Miss Winifred, Miss Isabella," he tried again. "We'll tell you what we learned, but first may I suggest *you sit down*?"

Agnes listened. She plunked herself on the sofa. "Winnie, Bella, sit down and let Drew speak." When they did so, grumbling, she turned to their brother. "Go on."

He sketched what they'd done overnight. Felix filled in details when his friend paused now and then for a jaw-cracking yawn. "And today I'll call on Ilsa and form a plan, *with her*, about what to do," he finished with a stern look at his sisters.

"She's leaving town," said Agnes.

Her brother shook his head. "She mustn't. I'll talk to her about that."

"Talk!" Winnie shot back to her feet. "Is that all?"

St. James stifled another yawn behind one hand. "What

would you have me do, Winnie? Run my sword through the sheriff?"

"Would you?" asked Bella hopefully.

"So they can both go to jail?" Agnes frowned at her.

"There must be *something*." In frustration Winnie turned on Felix. "File a suit!"

"On what grounds?"

"It's—it's harassment!"

"Aye," said Felix, "and perfectly legal if the sheriff suspects her of a crime."

"She *ought* to leave town," declared Bella as her sister gasped.

"No," repeated her brother. "That would be very unwise."

"Then you must stop her! Now!"

St. James sighed and gave Bella a weary look. "I'm trying..."

Winnie threw up her hands. "Men! Talk, talk, talk. Why have you got swords if you won't use them for anything important?" She headed for the door, Bella scurrying after her.

"Agnes," implored Felix. She paused, looking at him in apology, then ran after her sisters.

For a moment both men just stared at the empty doorway. "Bloody saints," said St. James blankly. He grabbed his boots and lurched back into his room.

Felix followed. As St. James splashed water on his face and scrambled into his clothes, Felix stuffed a change of garments into a rucksack, holding it out as his friend buckled on his sword. "In case," he said.

"You think she'll flee today? Now?" St. James slung the sack over his shoulder.

"I think that's why Agnes went with them. *She* thinks so."

"Are you coming?" His friend was already striding toward the door.

"Nipping at your heels."

The door slammed, and Felix rushed to get dressed.

When he reached the Ramsay house, a carriage was pulling away. The three St. James girls stood outside the house watching it go, clutching each other. At the sight of him, Agnes ran to his side. "We couldn't stop her, but Drew got into the carriage with her."

He nodded. "I knew he would."

"You did? Why?"

Felix looked at her. She was beautiful in the morning sunlight, her hair tumbling loose and shining like onyx, her eyes so anxiously hopeful. "Because he's in love with her and he'll stop at nothing to help her." He gave her a faint, lopsided smile. "I know how that feels."

Her glorious blue eyes widened as her sisters joined them. "What happened last night?" demanded Winnie. "Drew wouldn't tell us anything."

"You didn't give him much chance," Felix pointed out.

Winnie gasped, and Bella cried, "Oh, do tell us, Mr. Duncan. Why didn't he stop her?"

"I believe he will. No doubt they'll be home for dinner tonight. Give him time to hear her out and reason with her." He held up his hands as they all began to protest. "And I will tell you all that passed last night. Might I entreat you to join me for breakfast while I do?" He caught Agnes's eye. "Agnew's coffeehouse makes the most delicious currant buns."

"Yes, please!" Bella perked up.

"May we, Agnes?" put in Winnie eagerly. "What will Mama say?"

Felix watched Agnes, who stood gazing at him with adoration. God how he loved her.

"Of course," she said softly to her sister's question. "Mama won't mind, when she hears we're with Mr. Duncan. She knows we can trust him."

Chapter Fifteen

✿

Agnes had believed that when Drew returned to town, he would resolve everything.

The one point he had been firm on was that Ilsa should not leave town, and Agnes was certain he would convince Ilsa to turn around and come home. He'd had to run to catch it, but he'd managed to throw himself inside Ilsa's carriage. It was only a matter of time before he persuaded her to turn around.

Felix answered their questions over currant buns and tea in Agnew's, but by now Agnes knew him well enough to sense that there was something he didn't tell. After he had walked them to the shop, she lingered outside to ask.

He glanced sideways at her. "What makes you think I didn't tell all?"

"Because I know you," she said. "You wouldn't want to alarm Winnie and Bella." He just shook his head, his expression questioning. Agnes tilted her head and touched his neckcloth, which was crooked. "And because you always needed to order more coffee when one of us asked a particularly pointed question, and then somehow the subject got changed, and you managed never to answer the question."

Now he looked startled. "Did I?" He frowned and stroked his chin. "I'm sure I didn't… I slept barely an hour last night, lass, take pity on a weary man…"

"Felix," she said softly. "Tell me."

He covered her hand, on his chest, with his. "Don't tell them," he murmured, flicking a glance toward the shop, where her sisters were visible through the window. "The sheriff agreed not to arrest Mrs. Ramsay, but he insists upon questioning her again. Your brother agreed to persuade her to stay in town and to *ask* her to speak to the sheriff again—in his presence," he added quickly as Agnes's mouth fell open.

"She won't want to…"

Felix squeezed her hand. "And you think he'll let them hound her? Drew, who will be the almighty Duke of Carlyle and Earl of Crieff and endless other titles and has already seen how powerful a cudgel that is?" Reluctantly Agnes smiled, and Felix grinned.

She went into the shop with a lighter heart. Felix was right; Drew would rectify everything. He'd always had a knack for persuading people. He was in love with Ilsa, and she with him. And he had that damned dukedom hovering around him like a cloud of golden dust, transforming even the most obdurate officials into helpful sycophants. Everything was going to be fine.

Thus, she was taken entirely off guard by the arrival of two sheriff's officers at the shop, wanting to know where her brother was.

Winnie and Agnes instinctively went silent. Their mother darted a glance at them; they had told her all about the morning. "I do not know, sir," Mama answered.

The officer, a surly fellow called Hay, glared at her. "Did he not tell you where he was going?"

"He's a grown man," she replied calmly. "He's not kept me informed of his whereabouts these dozen years or more."

The other officer, Mr. Middleton, smiled. "Of course not. But you must have some idea. Perhaps you, Miss St. James?"

Agnes kept perfectly still and answered truthfully. "None at all."

"You were there when he left," he pointed out in the same friendly tone. "You and your sisters."

Behind her, Winnie sucked in her breath. Agnes gripped her sister's hand to keep her silent. "We were there, sir, but none of us thought he intended to leave. He only returned to town late last night, you see."

Mr. Middleton nodded. "Perhaps your friend Mrs. Ramsay told you." He paused, still smiling but his eyes sharp. "You called on her yesterday, after all."

Agnes's heart stuttered. The sheriff *had* been watching Ilsa's house. "She said nothing to me of any travel plans."

"What did you discuss?"

She lifted her chin, gazing coolly at Mr. Hay for his belligerent question. "We spoke of how unjust it is to punish one person for the actions of another."

His face went red. Mama cleared her throat. "Neither my daughters nor I knew the captain had left town. Thank you for informing me. I won't lay his place at supper tonight. Now, if you'll be so kind, good sirs, we have patrons." She smiled in that steely, polite way that always wrung compliance from her children.

Mr. Middleton took it gracefully and left. Mr. Hay's jaw twitched and he glared at all of them before he followed his fellow officer.

Slowly Mama turned. "Did you know?"

Agnes and Winnie both shook their heads. Felix had *insisted* Drew would convince Ilsa to stay.

Mama turned to gaze out the windows. "Let us hope Andrew knows what he's doing."

. . .

THE OFFICERS also caught Felix unawares, because he was fast asleep. After escorting the St. James ladies to Shakespeare Square, he'd gone straight home and collapsed into bed, vaguely expecting Drew would be there when he woke.

Instead, Callum roused him with the news that two steaming angry sheriff's deputies were in his sitting room, demanding answers.

He scrubbed the sleep from his face and racked his tired brain. If they wanted to see *him*, then St. James had either disappeared or done something dreadful.

When he went into the sitting room, a big fellow all but swung at him. "Where is he?" snarled the man without preamble.

Felix stood where he was. He'd learned as a young skinny lad never to give ground in the face of an angry, bigger boy. "Who, pray?"

"Captain St. James," said Mr. Middleton. He was one of the officials Felix and Drew had spoken to late last night. "Do you know where he's gone?"

Felix frowned. "Gone? What do you mean?"

"He left town this morning with Mrs. Ramsay," said Middleton. "Where did they go? Mr. Hay and I require a word with him."

"Goodness," Felix murmured instead of what he wanted to say, which was extremely profane. So much for an entire night's worth of insisting to officials that Ilsa Ramsay had done nothing wrong, wasn't *going* to do anything wrong, knew nothing about her father's actions or whereabouts, and didn't deserve to be treated like a criminal. Last night he and St. James had agreed it would be madness for her to leave town. He'd been sure his friend would convince her.

"As you know, sir, Mrs. Ramsay may have information regarding her father, who is wanted for questioning. Obstructing our inquiry would be a serious offense."

"So I ask again, where is he?" demanded Hay.

"I've no idea," said Felix in surprise. "Why would I?"

Middleton's smile grew thin. "Come, Mr. Duncan."

"He assured me that he meant to advise Mrs. Ramsay to stay in Edinburgh. He'd only just returned from three weeks at Fort George, you see, and had had no communication with her in that time. When he reached town late yesterday, he was greatly alarmed to hear what Mrs. Ramsay had been subjected to."

Middleton cleared his throat. "Then why did he get into a carriage with her this morning and leave?"

"You make it sound like conspiracy, when I know he had to chase down the carriage."

Hay scowled. "So he didn't intend to go?"

Felix shrugged. "He's at perfect liberty to go where he chooses. He's not under any suspicion."

"He is now," snapped Hay.

"Of what?" Felix fixed a steady gaze on him.

"Aiding a criminal."

"Mrs. Ramsay hasn't been arrested or charged with any crime."

"She's a witness!"

"She was in Perth when half the robberies happened. Hard to witness anything from fifty miles away."

Hay's face was redder than ever. "She knows where her father's gone."

"And you have proof of that?" Felix knew they didn't, but he still held his breath.

Middleton held up both hands. "Nay, sir, we only want to speak to her."

"You have, several times. You've read the letter she received from her father. The procurator's office admits it contains no helpful information. Is it not possible—even likely—that she knows nothing, and has grown so weary of being suspected that she's left town for more peaceful surroundings?" He smiled slightly. "Who knows—perhaps they decided to elope. The captain is extraordinarily attached to the lady."

Middleton understood, Felix saw. If St. James married Mrs. Ramsay, the sheriff couldn't arrest her. The same clout that got St. James the lord advocate's ear, and into the deputy procurator's house at two in the morning, would keep his wife out of jail—out of the sheriff's reach entirely.

Hay swore. "We understand you, sir. Thank you for your *help*." He spat out the last word and stormed from the room.

Middleton gave Felix a thoughtful look. "If you have any sway with Captain St. James, you would do well to remind him of the promises he made last night."

"If I had any idea where to find him," said Felix honestly, "I would."

After the sheriff's men left, he sagged into a chair. *What the bloody hell, Drew?* he thought irritably. The plan had been to persuade Ilsa to stay put and engage an attorney to lodge a grievance with the sheriff's office over their surveillance of her. Drew meant to stand by her publicly and demonstrate to Edinburgh that she was above reproach.

And, Felix suspected, he meant to propose. He hadn't dropped the suggestion of elopement lightly. St. James was desperately in love with Ilsa. Marrying the future Duke of Carlyle would put a stop to the most vicious gossip about her, and a move to England would cut it off entirely.

Instead, apparently, St. James had let Ilsa persuade *him*.

Which made her look even more suspicious.

Which would cloud St. James's name.

Which would leave the sheriff embarrassed, thwarted, and in desperate want of someone else to harass.

And there were only four people he could.

Felix leapt up and shouted for Callum to find him some clean clothes.

· · ·

Normally it was Bella's task to set the table, but tonight Agnes did it, laying out the best of everything and fussing over each piece critically.

Her mother bustled in with the silver candlesticks, two of the few family heirlooms that hadn't been sold. "I wish we'd had more notice!"

"He thought sooner was better," replied Agnes for the fifth time.

"I know." Mama stepped back and surveyed the table. "We'll not be shamed at any rate. You've done a lovely job, my dear."

"Didn't I, too?" protested Bella.

Mama smiled. "Of course, but Agnes has done an especially lovely job of it."

"We know why," murmured Winnie.

Agnes ignored them and went to check her hair again. She'd arranged it so carefully, but thought some of the pins had come loose. She hurried up the stairs to the round mirror over the basin on the landing.

She wore her favorite dress, the pale blue chemise à la reine with the white ruffle at the neckline. Her finger trembled as she touched a drop of scent on her throat.

The knocker sounded below. Normally she or one of her sisters would have answered it, but tonight Mama had stationed Annag there. Her heart thumping, Agnes hurried to the drawing room.

Felix entered first, his hair slicked back into a queue that shone like polished copper against his dark jacket. He stopped short at the sight of her.

Agnes smiled hopefully.

An answering grin spread over his face.

"Mr. Duncan, come in," said Mama.

"Thank you, ma'am." He bowed and stepped to the side. "Allow me to present my father, Lord Lachlan Duncan.

Father, this is Mrs. St. James and her daughters Miss Agnes St. James, Miss Winifred St. James, and Miss Isabella St. James."

The ladies curtsied. The gentlemen bowed. Agnes studied Felix's father with covert curiosity. Like his son, he was tall and spare, dressed in black except for his snowy white shirt and neckcloth. He wore a wig powdered gray, and his sharp blue eyes went right to her. Helplessly she froze, until a smile softened his face, and she beamed back.

Felix had suggested this. Actually he had proposed dinner at a tavern, but Mama overruled that on the spot. She understood at once what Felix was trying to achieve, and Agnes was slightly taken aback by how decisively Mama embraced it.

Be seen in company, Felix had urged them. *Do not hide yourself away from prying, hungry eyes. Glut them with your utter lack of concern and the gossip will wither away for lack of fuel.*

Because Drew, it appeared, had run off with Ilsa Ramsay. No one had expected that—quite the opposite, in fact—but both were gone, the sheriff was fuming, and now *they* teetered on the brink of being sucked into the growing scandal over Deacon Fletcher.

Thus had Felix offered up his father, an eminent and respected judge, as a dinner guest beyond reproach. It caused a flurry in Agnes's breast; she'd never met Felix's father. The one time he came to call, all those years ago, she'd been a child hiding on the stairs. This would be very different.

"It is a pleasure, madam," the judge told her mother. "Thank you for inviting us to share your table."

Mama was a little flushed. "We are so pleased to have you. Would you care for a glass of sherry?"

Under the sherry's influence, the formality faded quickly. The judge had a dry, laconic wit that made Mama laugh, and Winnie and Bella were quickly delighted as well. Agnes and Felix managed to end up standing side by side, watching their families together.

"Your father is charming," she whispered.

Felix grinned. "He can be."

Agnes laughed quietly. "Then he must be determined! Mama was worried. We've never had such an august personage to dine."

"Ah. Well," said Felix, lowering his voice even more, "Da was also concerned. He agreed at once when I proposed this." He paused. "In truth, he's been eager to make your acquaintance."

She glanced at him, startled.

Felix was watching her, his eyes lightning-hot. Agnes wondered if she would ever stop feeling his gaze like a caress, tempting and wicked. For a moment the rest of the room faded away, as if no one else existed but the two of them, yearning for each other...

"You're beautiful tonight," he breathed. His eyes dropped for a heartbeat. "That dress ought to be its own category of sin."

Agnes had to work to breathe. It was the same dress she'd worn That Night, when they'd been alone and lost in each other. She hadn't worn it since, and now she had wild thoughts of finding an excuse to drag him up to her tiny room and tear off the dress...

"Agnes," called Winnie, "come tell the story about Robert eating the golf ball! Did you know Lord Duncan is a golfer?"

Felix's eyes crinkled with wry amusement. He held out a hand to lead her back to the others, and Agnes took it, barely containing herself when his other hand ran boldly over her back, where no one could see.

There was no more chance of any privacy during dinner, even though Felix sat beside her. It was still the most enjoyable evening in a long while. Felix managed to touch her hand every time he passed her a dish, which set off sparks beneath her skin and questions in her mind.

It must mean something. He'd kissed her—many times

now—held her, implied that he loved her. He said his father wanted to meet her, and the judge had smiled at her very warmly.

When dinner was over, after another round of sherry and whisky, the Duncan gentlemen took their leave. Mama closed the door behind them, still smiling. "What a delightful evening."

"Aye," teased Winnie. "And a delightful gentleman!"

Mama waved one hand, her cheeks pink. "To bed with you, Winifred."

"What?" asked Winnie innocently. "I meant Mr. Duncan, of course." She stole a glance at Agnes. "Not that we didn't suspect as much, but it is so interesting to meet a gentleman's father and see what sort of man he'll be in a few decades."

"If that's so, then Mr. Duncan has nothing to worry about," said Bella. "Nor does Agnes."

"Bella!"

She widened her eyes. "What? Lord Duncan's a handsome old fellow."

"Old!" cried Mama.

"You know what I mean." Bella turned to Agnes. "I think you ought to snap him up. He's handsome, he's helped us so much, and his da is kind and amusing. And he has his own golf clubs! If you marry Mr. Duncan, we'd be able to play so much more often."

"I agree," said Winnie quickly. "Not about the golf, but about the rest, most certainly."

"Thank you for your advice." Agnes was torn between embarrassment and amusement.

Winnie beamed. "Now we've just got to hope Drew can persuade Ilsa to marry him, and all will be right with the world."

"Girls," scolded their mother.

Bella blinked at her. "Yes, Mama? Isn't is so pleasing to have love in the air? I daresay Lord Duncan looked at *you* very happily, perhaps his son isn't the only one in want of a wife."

"Ach!" Mama threw up her hands. "You silly child. To bed with you!"

Laughing, her sisters clattered up the stairs.

And Agnes noticed that no one, not even herself, had expressed any doubt whatsoever of her marrying Felix.

Chapter Sixteen

Taking his father to dine with the St. James ladies turned out to be a masterstroke.

Felix had decided to take the gamble when his network of legal gossip reported that the sheriff was sure the St. James family knew more than they were letting on about where Drew had gone, and the men who had watched Mrs. Ramsay's house moved to watch the St. James home instead.

His father was a willing collaborator, at his most charming the whole evening, making Mrs. St. James smile and the younger girls laugh. Felix saw how his father covertly eyed Agnes, and heard the extra gentleness in his tone when he spoke to her, but the judge was on good behavior and said nothing imprudent.

Until they left, that is. When they reached the street, Felix tipped his hat insolently to the sheriff's men lingering in a narrow close across the street. His father, on the other hand, walked straight over and spoke to them. He asked their names and purpose, instructed them to keep an eye out for any suspicious figures because the thieving ring was still an open case, and ended by saying he hoped he didn't see them in his courtroom on charges of harassment.

"You told me to be discreet," Felix said as Lachlan came back, leaving the officers bowing and scraping in his wake.

The judge raised his brows. "That was discreet. For their ears only."

Felix grinned. Word would get around the sheriff's office as fast as sound could travel.

They walked a minute before Lachlan said, "A very charming family."

"Aye."

"I remember the son," he went on. "A tall, dark-haired boy, always trying to keep you from trouble."

Felix choked. "Keep—! He joined in every prank and caper!"

Lachlan chuckled. "And I suspect I have finally solved the years-old mystery of the disappearing hams."

Felix started. He'd sent food anonymously to the St. Jameses for a few years after Drew refused to accept money and left for the army. He'd thought his father hadn't noticed. "They wouldn't accept any other help," he said, deciding there was no point in denying it.

His father shook his head. "I wouldn't have protested, if you'd asked me. The housekeeper was driven to despair."

"I ought to have told her."

"Aye. And speaking of things you *ought* to have done, why was I not able to welcome the young lady to our family tonight?"

Caught off guard, he flushed. "It doesn't feel right to ask her now."

The judge clucked in disapproval. "*Amor neminem praestolatur*, lad."

Felix clamped his jaw shut and walked faster. *Love waits for no one.* Perhaps not, but he'd made the worst marriage proposal of all time. He had a lot to overcome with his next one.

But searching for the right moment only grew harder.

Within days word filtered out that Drew had come to blows with some sheriff's men sent after them, which made Felix want to punch someone himself; what the blazes was Drew doing?

Drew and Ilsa did not return to Edinburgh. The sheriff's men remained outside the St. James home.

The strain grew evident in their household. Felix took to calling every day, both to keep an eye on the sheriff's men and to offer what little comfort he could. His sources of news ran dry; even his father heard nothing. He still went to see the ladies, who had begun to blame themselves.

"This is our fault, isn't it?" asked Bella tearfully. "We *badgered* Drew."

"He made his own decisions," Felix promised her. "He swore he would do anything in his power for her."

Winnie bit her lip. "He didn't want Ilsa to leave, but when she insisted, he went with her. Because we were standing there urging him on."

"I feel certain he would have gone regardless of your presence, if he couldn't persuade her to stay."

Another tear ran down Bella's face. Mrs. St. James reached for her, but Bella flinched away and ran out, followed closely by Winnie.

Her face pale, Louisa St. James turned to Felix. "Thank you, Mr. Duncan."

He squeezed his clasped hands. "I wish I had happier news to tell you."

"I know." Slowly, as if pained, she rose and left.

Felix looked at Agnes, sitting silent and stricken on the sofa. "Are you going to flee as well?"

She swallowed. "To where? There's nowhere to go to escape this, is there?"

Frustration boiled up inside him. He'd long since let go of any anger at St. James—after the surprise had worn off, Felix had realized he oughtn't to have been surprised at all. He'd once told Agnes he thought Ilsa Ramsay could change Drew's mind about leaving Scotland; of course she would be able to persuade him to go along on her mad and quixotic quest.

None of that could comfort the man's family. They feared for him, and for Ilsa.

"Put on your sturdy shoes and hat," he said abruptly. "Let's go."

Agnes blinked. "Where?"

The idea materialized in his head like a vision. "Out."

As MAD As the idea sounded, once they reached the park, Agnes inhaled deeply and felt her shoulders ease. It was a beautiful day, and she had missed the outdoors.

"Are you ready to climb?" Felix joined her, having settled with the driver of the hack.

She shielded her eyes and gazed up. Arthur's Seat, a bald mass of stone, towered seven hundred feet above them. "'Tis a rugged ascent."

"We have a picnic to eat on top." He swung a bulging rucksack over one arm and winked.

He must have bought it when he went out to hire the carriage while she changed clothes. Slowly Agnes smiled. "We'll want it!"

Almost three hours later they reached the pinnacle. The sun broke through the clouds in patches, and the breeze was calm. And it was deserted—not a single person on the path, nor at the summit. Energized and breathless from the climb, Agnes charged ahead, remembering, and after a search, found what she sought.

"A handsome perch," said Felix with a laugh as he caught up a few minutes later.

Agnes grinned down at him from the rocky outcropping she'd scrambled atop. "My father and I used to sit here. It offers the most beautiful view of Edinburgh."

"Aye," he agreed.

Agnes tilted up her face to the intermittent sun, letting her hat slide off to hang by its ribbons down her back. It was so good to be out of town, away from *everyone*. She had worried the sheriff's men would follow, but Felix said he'd told them where he and Agnes were going and pledged not to stray from Edinburgh. She hadn't realized how weighty their scrutiny was until now, when it was gone.

"This was my favorite place in the world," she said. "Drew went to school, my mother and sisters couldn't make the climb, so I had Papa to myself here."

"He was a good man," said Felix quietly.

"The best." A lump formed in her throat, thinking of Papa. "I'm not going to leave Edinburgh with Drew," she said abruptly.

From the corner of her eye, she saw his head whip around toward her.

"I understand that he must go," she went on when Felix said nothing. "Winnie and Bella are very excited to see London, which means Mama will go, too."

"But you don't wish to," he murmured.

She shook her head. "I love Edinburgh, even after... all this. Papa loved it, too."

"You don't feel he would want you to go with them?"

"No." She smiled ruefully. "Papa never wanted the slightest thing to do with Carlyle. My grandfather was the old duke's brother, and the duke threw him out when he was a young man. What family bans one of their own? No one from Carlyle ever spoke to my grandfather or my father again. They only want Drew now because they cannot keep him from inheriting, and they mean to shape him into their sort of man."

"They've not succeeded," said Felix. "Nor will they. He knows who he is."

Agnes nodded. "When he first came home and told us, I

feared they would change him—and us. But I was wrong."
She glanced at him. "We're a stubborn lot, St. Jameses."

He affected surprise. "Are you? No, surely not…"

She laughed. "I'm going to stay here and run the shop.
Papa bought it so we would always have an income, and I
intend to keep it when my family leaves. He would want
me to."

Felix just nodded, listening and watching her.

In the distance, far below and just barely visible, were the
cricket grounds where they had played. Where Papa had
taught her that everyone deserved a chance to play, as long as
they gave their best effort. That was what Papa had admired
most about Felix, she realized; he never gave up, and always
gave his all. Just as he'd done for her, and for Drew and Ilsa.
"He thought you were a good lad."

"Did he?" Felix smiled. "I used to wish my da was more
like your papa."

"But your father is charming!"

"To you," he retorted. "He's a bit harder on me."

"What would he think of me, running the shop when
Mama leaves?"

He winked. "That he likes a determined lass."

She laughed, then looked away. "What would you think
of it?"

"I? I admire anyone who strives hard for their heart's
desire. And I'm very fond of that shop now." He gave her a
sinful look. "I've been kissed fair out of my mind in the
salon."

She gasped, then burst out laughing and smacked his
shoulder. It put her off balance, and she gave a startled shriek
as she started to slide.

The ground was grassy. The stone ledge she sat on was
only a few feet high. But Felix caught her in his arms and held
her as if snatching her from the jaws of death.

"Thank you," she said breathlessly. Her arms had gone naturally around his neck.

His eyes crinkled up when he smiled. "Any time," he murmured, letting her feet back to the ground.

And then he kissed her. As always, it went to her head like whisky drunk too fast, making her feel giddy and beautiful and absolutely wild with wanting.

It had never been whisky that made her feel this way, though; it was *Felix*. Just him. Every time he kissed her. She hadn't understood until now that it had been the first sign they were meant to be together.

"Did you really want to marry me?" she managed to ask as he kissed her jaw. "When you asked."

"I did," he growled. "Enough that I rushed to do it against all advice."

Her eyes flew open in alarm. "Who advised against it?"

"Hmm." He squinted against the emerging sun, which gilded his hair to polished copper. "My father and my partner both suggested waiting until I didn't look like a corpse freshly dug up from the grave."

She gasped. "You did not!"

He gave a short laugh. "I felt like one! And then worse, after hearing your answer."

Agnes wet her lips and lowered her gaze to the knot of his neckcloth, which had gone askew. "I'm sorry for that." She couldn't help herself; she tugged the knot straight and smoothed the ends. "After all you've done for my family, for Drew and Ilsa, for me, I am appalled that I thought so little of you—"

He tipped up her chin with one finger. "Nothing I did was done out of guilt, or to try to change your mind. I helped a friend in need, aye? You, and your family, owe me nothing."

His eyes were so blue, and his face so handsome. And dear. And beloved. She was head over heels in love with him. From attraction and desire had grown friendship and affection, until he was the person she thought of first in any important moment. He was the one she hoped to see enter, every time a door opened. His was the only hand she wanted on hers, his arms the only ones around her. His voice, low and hot at her ear. His mouth on hers.

She gripped his hand, suddenly tongue-tied. "I—Felix, I—"

He waited, his mouth still curved in a rueful smile.

"If you were to ask me again," she blurted out, "my answer would be different."

The familiar blue flame kindled in his eyes. "Agnes St. James," he exclaimed, "are you asking me to ask you to marry me?"

She blushed. "If you want to."

"Aye, I do," he murmured. "Have you any advice on how to do it?"

Agnes gulped, too anxious to laugh. "I love you."

The merriment dropped from his face.

She nodded, her throat too tight with nerves to say it again.

His eyes closed for a moment. "Will you marry me?" She started nodding, and he seized her for a fierce kiss. "Will you?" he demanded. "Truly?"

"Yes." She began to smile. "Yes. Did you think I would say *I love you* otherwise?"

He grinned, his fingers tightening on her jaw. "I've been falling in love with you since you tormented me by licking butter off your lips in Agnew's coffeehouse. I'll never stop falling for you, Agnes."

Her lips parted in astonishment, and he kissed her again, bearing her back against the rocky ledge. She wound her arms around him; there was no reason not to, now. Her heart felt full to bursting, her blood seemed to fizz in her veins, and her skin tingled everywhere.

She leaned back, arching her neck to feel the sun on her

face. The stone at her back, the fresh air around her, and Felix in front of her, his weight unbearably arousing against her. *I'll never stop falling for you*, echoed his voice over the drumming of her heart.

She reached out and pulled the tie holding his hair. Coppery waves fell over his shoulders and Agnes plunged in both hands, fascinated. He growled and made short work of the pins in her hair, wrapping the length around one big hand as he crowded closer and bared her throat to his sensual assault.

On instinct her legs parted. He pressed closer still. Wordless, she gripped his head as he lowered his mouth to the swells of her breasts and tasted her skin. Sensation rioted through her. She didn't even know she'd put her legs around his hips until he slipped one hand beneath her and hiked her higher, rocking his own hips against hers at the same time.

This must be a dream...

No... It's too good...

It was real. He was hers, and she was his, just as she had always wanted.

"I want you," she breathed. "Felix."

He huffed out a strained laugh. "Ye know I want *you*—always will, anywhere, beyond all reason."

She smiled fiercely, and shoved his jacket off his shoulders. He blinked, startled, then yanked it off. Her pulse accelerating, she untied her half cloak and let it fall it aside. For the shop she dressed fashionably, but today, for their walk, she wore a sturdy woolen skirt with a simple bodice. Much more suited to hiking.

Much easier to take off.

Felix's gaze burned like flame as she yanked off the kerchief and tugged out the first pin in her bodice. "Are ye tryin' tae kill me?" he asked, his Scots broad and deep.

"No." She pulled out another pin. "I'm trying to make love to you."

"Here?" he exclaimed, nonetheless following her as she backed away toward the picnic blanket he had already spread out in a sheltered spot behind the stone.

"Aye." Another pin came out. She stabbed it carefully next to the others in the peplum of her bodice. "Just the two of us, alone in the most beautiful spot in the world, with my papa smiling down on me for choosing a good lad for my husband."

His eyes flicked up to the sky. "Lightning might strike me…"

She laughed and removed the last pins. "Wouldn't it be worth it?"

Felix watched as she peeled off the bodice, exposing her stays and shift. She untied her skirt and stepped out of it.

"Aye." He yanked at his neckcloth. "It would be."

She laughed at him, and then shrieked with more laughter as he tackled her to the picnic blanket, pinning her flat beneath him. "Mo ghràdh," he whispered, his fingers spearing through hers as he dragged her arms above her head. He ducked his head and sucked lightly at the skin below her ear, making her quiver with longing.

"Felix," she gasped, writhing, wanting to touch him as much as he touched her.

"Here now." His voice was deep and rough, which made her burn inside. "Don't rush me…"

"I'm dying of wanting you," she confessed. "Always have been. Why do you think I begged you to do such things to me at the Assembly Rooms?" There was no reason to keep it from him, not now.

His face grew taut. Thin white lines bracketed his mouth. "Yer tryin' to kill me," he growled. "Ye want me to ride you hard and fast?"

"Yes," she whimpered, pushing her hips upward into his.

"And ye want me to make you come again and again, here on this hillside?"

"Yes," she moaned, her insides molten at the thought.

"And ye want me to leave us both spent and exhausted from pleasure?" He bit—bit!—the tender skin at the curve of her neck, and Agnes almost sobbed her answering, "*yes*."

He made her wait for it. With his hands and with his mouth, he undressed her to her stockings. He brought her to one climax before he even removed his boots. He worshipped her body, murmuring Scots endearments as she recovered from the heady thrill of it—laving her breasts until she thought she would weep, tormenting her with his hand between her legs as he tasted every inch of her body until she cried out in release.

She still shuddered from that release when he finally flung off the last of his clothes. "When shall we be married?" He moved over her, his hair wild and glowing in the sunlight.

"Tomorrow," she gasped, reaching for him.

He caught her hand and pressed it to his lips for a kiss. "Not soon enough. I take thee for my wedded wife here and now." He spread her legs far apart and stroked her there, his touch sure and bold. Agnes thought she might go up in literal flames as her body responded once more.

"I take you," she managed, arching her neck as he did it again.

"Mine, to love and to cherish," he rasped, and then he pushed inside her. Her body was so soft and pliant it didn't hurt. No, it felt good—so good—like a missing piece fitting into place, smooth and thick and hot, bearing into her until her flesh molded to his. She thrashed her head, speechless.

He lowered himself over her, his weight holding her still. "I'm yours forever," he breathed in her ear. He nipped her earlobe, making her spasm. "And you're mine, 'til death do us part."

She seized his face in both hands and kissed him. With a moan, he began to move, each thrust jolting and awakening her. God how she wanted him—how she wanted this— She pulled up her knees and curled her legs around his waist, wordlessly begging him for more, harder, faster. Her heart was racing as if it would explode. She gripped his shoulders and squeezed her eyes shut, plummeting toward rapture like a stone dropped from a cliff.

With a harsh sound Felix pushed himself up on one arm. He cupped her cheek and moved, hard and relentless against her, his expression fierce and focused. Agnes came with a gasp and burst into sobs.

Felix gave a shout, shuddering against her, his weight falling forward. Incoherent, still sobbing, Agnes reached for him, and he folded her into his shaking arms, rolling them to the side. His chest heaving, his skin damp with sweat, he kissed her forehead and clasped her to him. After a moment he pulled his discarded kilt over them, and Agnes curled against him, blissfully worn out and sated.

"Now you have to marry me," he said after a while. His fingers were running through her hair, making her want to fall asleep right where she was.

She smiled against his bare chest. Copper hairs tickled her cheek, and on a whim she touched her tongue to his nipple, pale pink and rigid. He twitched, to her pleasure. "Because you ruined me?"

"Nay, lass." His hand flexed on the curve of her hip. "You've ruined *me*. Lightning might have struck me and I wouldn't have noticed."

She laughed. "'Tis a good thing I want to marry you, then. I'll expect this sort of treatment every day."

"Glory be to God above," he growled.

Agnes laughed again. "Felix..." She ran her fingers over his chest, marveling at how solid and strong he was. "What do you think Drew and Ilsa are doing?"

"Something like this, I wouldn't doubt."

Another burst of happiness glowed inside her. "So you think he'll marry her?"

He shifted his arm beneath her. "He wants to."

"I hope he does." She gazed up at the sky, absently stroking his chest.

"As long as he doesn't give me any grief, I will wish him very happy."

She raised her head and propped her chin on his shoulder to look him in the face. He had turned white, that day long ago, when she mentioned her brother. "You think he won't approve?"

He grinned lazily. "You'd better marry me soon, just in case. He can't shoot his brother-in-law."

She gasped, then giggled, and soon they were holding each other, laughing helplessly. It was so lovely to be here, relaxed and easy, with him. Felix had known exactly what she needed—what they both needed. Fresh air, sunshine, a perfect moment to confess their love.

So much love, she didn't know how one person could hold so much feeling inside herself.

This would be her favorite place on earth forever.

Epilogue

❦

I t was a simple matter, telling her family. Her mother took one look at her face and smiled.

"Have you some news for us, Agnes dear?"

Blushing, smiling so wide her cheeks hurt, Agnes nodded.

"Oh! Mr. Duncan!" screamed Winnie, bounding over to throw her arms around Agnes. "I knew it, I knew it!"

"At last," cried Bella. "Oh, Agnes!"

Laughing, she embraced her sisters. "Yes, Mr. Duncan."

"Where shall you be married? In St. Giles? Mama, we must have new gowns!"

"Now if only Drew marries Ilsa." Bella sighed in joy. "See, Mama, everything is coming out right."

Mama wagged a finger at her, but Bella proved correct. A few days later Drew and Ilsa reappeared in Edinburgh, weary and travel-stained. There was bad news—Ilsa's father had disappeared, feared never to be found—but also good news: they had married in Glasgow. The St. James household rang once more with joyful cries. And when Drew visited the sheriff and the procurator-fiscal, looking once more like the heir to a dukedom, it ended with both apologizing to Ilsa for the distress they had caused her.

Agnes and Felix were married a fortnight later with their families in attendance. Mama surprised Agnes on the morning of the wedding with a new gown of pale pink satin, embroidered all over with small white flowers. "I put this bolt aside weeks ago. I knew it was for you the moment I saw it in the warehouse," Mama confided.

"It's beautiful!" She hesitated, holding the beautiful gown against her. "Mama—about the shop…"

"Yes, I know." Her mother smiled ruefully. "You want the shop, now that Andrew is taking us to England." She sighed. "And of course you shall have it. Papa would want that. He knew you hoped to run it, someday."

"He did?"

Mama laughed. "Well, he never thought Andrew would stand there talking about fine silks! And you've earned it, my dear. Papa would be very proud of you—as am I. But will your Mr. Duncan understand?"

Agnes blushed. She had already discussed everything with her future husband. "Felix understands."

Drew walked her to the altar. No matter how she tried to pay attention, Agnes barely heard a word of the service. And then it was over, with a gold ring on her finger, her sisters chattering happily, Mama wiping away a tear, and Ilsa beaming at her. Lord Duncan kissed her forehead and pronounced himself thoroughly pleased. And Felix…

He gazed at her with love in his eyes, until a sly smile curved his mouth and he gave her a wicked wink that made her blush from head to toe.

"Oh no! But this means you won't come to London with us!" cried Winnie

Agnes stole a glance at Felix. He raised his brows expectantly. "No," she told her sister. "I've found my happy ever after in Scotland."

And this time, the wicked wink was hers.

About this Story

Originally the St. James sisters were minor characters in their brother's story, but they kept stealing the scenes. So did Drew's smart-mouthed friend Felix. By the time I got to the maze scene in the novel, I knew I was going to write about Agnes and Felix.

If you'd like to know how Drew met Ilsa, kissed her in the maze, haunted an attic with her, and what they did when they ran off at the end in search of her father, that story is told in A SCOT TO THE HEART.

Thank you for reading!

If you enjoyed the story, I hope you'll consider leaving a review or rating online to help other readers.

For access to special previews, exclusive giveaways, and my very latest news, join my VIP Readers list at www.carolinelinden.com. New members get a free exclusive short story as a welcome gift.

About the Author

Caroline Linden was born a reader, not a writer. She earned a math degree from Harvard University and wrote computer software before turning to writing fiction. Since then the Boston Red Sox have won the World Series four times, which is not related but still worth mentioning. Her books have won the NEC Reader's Choice Award, the Daphne du Maurier Award, the NJRW Golden Leaf Award, and RWA's RITA Award, and have been translated into seventeen languages. She lives in New England.

CPSIA information can be obtained
at www.ICGtesting.com
Printed in the USA
LVHW081131030722
722671LV00028B/819